The Vast and Gruesome Clutch of Our Law

By B. C. Bamber

'THE VAST AND GRUESOME CLUTCH OF OUR LAW'

Published by Vagabond Unlimited
Copyright © B.C.Bamber 2011

Vagabond Unlimited, Montpellier House, Montpellier Drive, Cheltenham.
Gloucestershire, GL50 1TY
info@mediamight.co.uk

First Edition 2004
Second Edition 2006
Third Edition (EBook) 2010
Fourth Edition 2011

ISBN: 0-9549691-7-0

*Dedicated to Dominic, Glen, Hilary, Daniel, Ronald,
Nick, Zoe, Dave and especially to John Walker, John Wood
and Doug.*

'She saw the gypsy twice. Once he came to the house, with things to sell. And she, watching him from the landing window, refused to go down. He saw her, too, as he was putting his things back into his cart. But he too gave no sign. Being of a race that exists only to be harrying the outskirts of our society, forever hostile and living only by spoil, he was too much master of himself, and too wary, to expose himself openly to the vast and gruesome clutch of our law.'

D. H. Lawrence; 1930; P.74

Part One: Goscote's End

CHAPTER ONE

The Governor stared out of the window overlooking Goscote. All he could do was watch, aimlessly and helplessly, as the town decayed and the residents died one by one. It was now thirty years since the cloud arrived; seventy years of decline had led here. He could see most of the town from his window. The buildings that would have been filled with life, now empty. Ruins of a town known for its vibrancy and cleanliness spread out for a couple of miles, the population now living in just one building, which he could see from the back window. But for now he looked out across the town, just a metre or two from the ledge, the rusty iron frame showing through the concrete. He could throw himself off right now and end it all.

Paint was peeling off the walls, the brickwork crumbling. The cars and buses, trucks, and the odd rusting shell of a bike, strewn randomly across the main street. The Governor lived in a building showing the same signs of neglect. He scratched his beard, and in a hopeless daze he thought how this town was once a regional power. A well planned, clean, important place, before the country began its dramatic economic collapse.

The Governor was in his late sixties, tall and thin. His belt held his trousers together, which hung off his hips. He had to keep tugging at them to keep them up. He did not command a team of staff. He didn't have a large car and a reserved parking space, or a generous expense account. He wasn't given any special privileges as Governor, apart from this crumbling house and a large desk with a leather top. His respect from the people there was given, rather than earned. The administrational aspects of his position had long since given way to the lack of people, along with lack of resources, and recently, even the shortage of pens, pencils and paper. His assistant, Edward, was twenty-one and the second most powerful man in town.

He was the Governor's primary adviser and counsel. Not that either of them enjoyed power. In reality, the older residents commanded more respect than they did.

The population had levelled off at one hundred and thirty, the last child having been born three years ago to Edward and his wife Madeline. Edward was thin, as they all were. He was five foot eleven, and gangly, pale-looking, with a cold intelligent stare. Wise for his years.

Edward crept in and stood unseen behind the Governor, who was still staring out of the same window, watching the birds circling around in the sky outside the fifth floor.

The Governor spoke. 'It's failed.'

Edward was startled by his sudden sentence, unaware that the Governor knew he was there. Edward wondered for a second whether the Governor was talking to himself, and remained silent, checking around to make sure there was no one else in the room. Cruelly, he wanted to see the Governor like this, perhaps doubting whether he was properly handling the suffering of the last of the people here. Edward was like the others, questioning what good he was doing. But he knew that for the people to depose the Governor was as good as Edward himself being deposed.

'We could have had a burst of activity, increased our crop yields, and invented some kind of revival. But we didn't. At least I didn't, as it was…is my responsibility… .' He paused and looked round. 'Edward.' The Governor turned his head, fully looking at his counsellor, stretching his neck as best he could without physically moving his entire body to face him, not entirely finished wistfully gazing out the window.

'Yes,' he replied, sharply.

The Governor was in possession of his faculties after all. He turned away again. He had noticed Edward creep in. Maybe he had misjudged him. Everyone was saying he should retire and let someone else take over, but Edward wanted him to stay on. The people were pretty genteel. He wasn't worried about being beaten to death or sent away. More that he enjoyed his job. There was more than ten years of family tradition to the job of Counsel to the Governor for Edward. It would be a wrench to have to give it up.

Edward had no doubt the Governor was a smart man. But the events of the last seven decades had everyone foxed, even the most intelligent among them.

'I thought you were there'. The Governor addressed Edward again. Edward could hear it in his voice, a little self-satisfaction that he'd not been outdone. 'I was worried I was talking to myself for a minute.' The Governor turned to face Edward properly. 'You think we've failed, Edward?' The insecurity crept back in again.

'Yes...I mean no. We haven't failed. Nature has failed us, Governor.' Edward smiled, quickly straightening his face afterwards.

The Governor sighed. He walked across to his chair and let himself drop into the seat. Plumes of dust lifted up from beneath him and quickly settled again. The dust made a mockery of him. Edward would have laughed, but knew that if he thought anything of the Governor, he'd ignore it. He would have to pretend that a governor would not be treated badly, even by the dust settling around him. But it was pretty hard to ignore, as Edward's nose began to itch.

The room, once filled with fine furniture, was now old and falling apart, rescued from the houses of the rich, and the old government buildings of Goscote. One chair was even received as a peace offering, when hostilities ceased with Goscote's neighbours, themselves in serious decline, if not already wiped out by the events that had hit Britain.

'Even the nomadic groups have stopped turning up. I reckon they must have settled down. Humanity has just about died out,' the Governor said, with a little resentment, resigned even to miss troublesome gypsies.

Edward offered some optimism. 'I think it will be one more generation and then things will begin to improve.' Edward smiled again, his thoughts elsewhere. 'Sir, I have to go soon. Madeline is expecting me.' He waited for a polite reprieve from duty, not that the Governor could stop him if he wanted to leave right there and then. But Edward's sense of duty remained.

The Governor grimaced, sighed, and gave Edward his leave, waving his hand. Edward, recognising immediately the signs of a man more comfortable in his own company, turned on his heels and silently walked out of the room, taking the stairs a few at a time, out into the frost-covered streets. Empty streets. He walked with enthusiasm, breaking into a run.

It was a short distance to the Town Hall, where the large majority of the town's people lived. The hall was through the grand front entrance, and once inside there were several balconies. Off to each side were the old offices of a once large local council. The room was full of beds and the small things people had kept. Lamps and ornaments, collections of clothing and odds and ends saved from their old houses. Family heirlooms mostly. Gathering dust, as with everything else they owned. They stayed together after years of raids, illnesses, and sudden deaths: for company and strength in numbers. The Town Hall had provided enough shelter and security for all of them. It was a hard building to break into. There were small rooms, to provide modest apartments for almost everyone, with a large grand flight of stairs at each side of the hall. For the last twenty years it was a communal home, now having successfully attracted the entire population into its protection. Its warm atmosphere produced a homely, comforting environment, where this struggling religious community could live out its life in peace. The people were no longer strangers. Hostility and crime were non-existent. They huddled together like this and it worked well. They could keep an eye on each other, and close the doors to the harsh world around them when needed. Everyone had great affection for this old building; a community, a fortress and a home.

Edward strode in. His tall thin frame and long legs raced up the large flight of stairs that swept round to a corridor, onto the first floor and in to see Madeline and their son Simon. He walked in as Madeline looked up in pleasant surprise, a smile on her face as he kissed them both, first Madeline, then Simon in quick succession. That permanent smile on his face, he sat down with a bump. Madeline was enjoying this period of happiness in Edward.

'What's the news then, Edward?' Madeline asked. She was dressed in a flowing skirt, her dark eyes and hair, her small pale face, the lines around her smile, giving Edward a warm glow, always happy to be in her company.

'What's the news? There isn't any, Madie.' Edward really didn't have any news. No reason to feel as happy as he seemed.

'You've got that look about you.' She smiled, looking at him, expecting something. Expecting him to give it up, whatever it was. A piece of unexpected news, perhaps, that he was keeping quiet about until the appropriate time. Edward could see that she suspected he had a secret. They just smiled at each other, in a knowing way. An unspoken game woven into their struggle for power in their marriage. A game most couples play, sometimes in a light hearted way, but more often a fierce battle for dominance. And he had been in a good mood for a while. A happy mood, out of context with their circumstances. He sat down and they chatted and played with Simon as he tottered around, getting into mischief.

Come nine o'clock Edward slipped out and strode back through the hall's double doors, into the cold, and across the street, clutching his coat around him with one arm, holding an oil lamp with the other. He crossed Broad Street, cut through two large buses, rusting where they had been parked for over a decade. He strolled up an alley and turned down into another, the lamp lighting his way, though he knew where to go by now, despite the darkness. The large dark building, which ran along the alley, loomed in its seven storeys, with large windows, many of which were broken or missing. He came back into Eddington Street, the second main road in Goscote. His coat curling behind him, he turned gracefully into the entrance, through the door, quickly poking his head back through to check he wasn't being followed. He ran up the stairs, two steps at a time, up to the fifth floor, moving through the double swing doors and into a large office. He passed empty desks, old phones and asset-stripped office supplies, as the doors swung back and forth for a while before closing. He walked straight to the far left of the room, into a longer room, and to a bed with a screen to minimise the draught. Also there was a telescope, resting on its tripod, pointing randomly into the sky. He took the telescope and panned across the skyline, as he had done most days. Then he looked down across Goscote, to see if anyone had seen him enter.

He did have a secret from Madie. She was right, as usual. But rather than a lie or a surprise of some kind, all he had to hide was this place. He came here to get away from things, and primarily to think about a plan to save his community. Also he watched for raiders, though they never came.

He held a collection of documents charting history and technology over the centuries that he'd rescued from the fires and furnaces. He kept the archive hidden in a large central room, the entrance covered up by a metal stationery cupboard. It wasn't well hidden, but no one knew he came here. He wanted to design a plan, but in all the time he'd been coming here, he'd come up with nothing.

All he had with him was a telescope, a bed, a notepad and pencil, and the archive. The telescope was given to him by his teacher, Mr Taylor, long since passed on. He was an elderly man, by the time he had come to teach Edward. In class he had brought the telescope in to show the children the dark cloud that covered almost half the planet, blotting out much of the sun for much of the year. Its shadow influencing all of their history since its arrival. In that lesson he had shown such enthusiasm for the telescope. That day in class, at seven years old, he had experienced something mysterious, which had guaranteed his interest in the study of the cloud ever since. When Mr Taylor died, he left it to Edward.

Eleven years ago, he had waited impatiently for his turn to use the telescope, his excitement charging the enthusiasm in class. Edward remembered how agonising it was waiting. Mr Taylor lined up the children to have a look at the cloud, his long grey beard adding to the illusion that the telescope was some fantastic piece of technology. In recognition of the agony of waiting, Mr Taylor kept the line moving. He believed in an idea that Edward now shared, that their salvation would come as soon as that cloud had gone. It kept the Earth dark and cold for ten months of the year. Not old enough or big enough to look unaided, like the bigger children, he had stepped up for his turn, climbing up on a crate. First he looked at the mountains across the plain, a mile out of town. A dark construction of peaks and valleys, lined up across the skyline. Instructed by his teacher, he lifted the telescope and looked at the cloud. As he did so, a voice said, 'Keep looking.' A whisper. A kind voice, which he knew had not come from the people in the room, shocking the words into him. He remembered his heart jumping at the sound. He climbed down, feeling frightened, instinctively knowing its significance. He quietly moved back, disturbed by it all and yet fascinated. He kept quiet about it, until he eventually told Mr Taylor, who suggested he should not tell his family that he had heard this voice, for fear of what they might say. Mr Taylor did not want the rest of his young life determined by one instance of voice-hearing. He would keep a close eye on the lad and that's how their friendship started. Thinking back, Mr Taylor was probably just as intrigued. Just as desperate to know the fate of Britain and the rest of the world, as Edward was.

Over the rest of the three years under the tutelage of Mr Taylor, he had consistently asked to use the telescope. Edward and the aging Mr Taylor often discussed the cloud's devastating impact on the world. This and a combination of wars and economic decline had all but killed off the world's peoples and cultures. A general history of seventy years of declining and dying human life. This knowledge had been passed down to young Edward over those years, eventually leaving him the telescope so that he could continue his wait for a sign that the voice he heard was the truth speaking. A Godly message of hope that something or someone was coming to move that cloud from its place, holding humanity to its silent rule.

His hideout had been operational for a year and a half. Most of his friends accepted his wanderings, just as they enjoyed his recent unexplained happiness. They had quickly come to rely on it. They were drawn to his mysterious cheerfulness. When things had been so bleak for such a long time, and the future so uncertain, a cheerful face was a hopeful thing. A precious commodity, at times as vital as fresh water and sunlight. They were glad of it. That is, all except Mrs Edmunds, always suspicious of him and the Governor.

Mrs Edmunds wasn't a bad person. She just didn't like the

Governor and she disliked Edward even more. His smiling face must have seemed as if he was mocking her, when there was so little to be happy about. She didn't understand the vital role of morale on survival. Edward did. That's why he was smiling. This was now the last generation of survivors, represented in part by Edward's son Simon. Edward felt certain that something would happen to stop their final end. That cloud was going to move. He was sure and the voice kept him looking.

CHAPTER TWO

Edward walked into the hall at breakfast. A mass of talkative people, all eating, noisily discussing all manner of things, the cutlery clattering and people going back and forth to the kitchen hatch. Drinks being served and vegetable soup, dripping from the ladles and spoons. The hall was big enough to have breakfast and other meals served at one end of it. The stage end had chairs set up for meetings, leaving enough room in the middle, which was mostly unused. Everyone was talking about a meeting to be held immediately after they had eaten. Edward listened as he sat down, adjusting his hearing and concentration to pick up the threads of conversation, listening for keywords to fill in the gaps he'd already missed. He quickly gathered the relevant information, from bits he overheard, and realised, not surprisingly, that they were discussing plans to challenge the Governor. A favourite topic of conversation led by the Mr Workman and Mrs Edmunds duo.

These elderly peers were the most politically active. They were a partnership, but not without their fair share of disagreements. Mr Workman was more moderate than Mrs Edmunds, who tended to be the militant voice in the community. Mr Workman tempered and counteracted her desire to make the Governor's life a misery. She was always looking for conflicts to be resolved, often inventing them to cause problems. Edward suspected she was an unhappy old woman with nothing better to do. She may be unhappy, but as Edward often explained to the Governor (who had little to do with her), she was more than capable of whipping up support for every tiresome little thing. The only person who could distract her enough for the issues to move on, was Mr Workman. He, on the other hand, only made issues audible when they were important, and for that reason he was often called upon to express an opinion and decide on many aspects of the community. Mr Workman was a good man, and he also had a great deal of time and respect for Mrs Edmunds. So the two worked effectively together. They were the real political power in Goscote, and everyone knew it.

They wanted more of a plan to help the dying town. More action or they were going to disappear. Eventually Mr Workman, now in his early seventies, stood up and called across to Edward, to ask him if he would ask the Governor to attend. His old face crinkling as he spoke, his head lifted up slowly, his nose in the air to carry his voice across the room.

'The Governor will attend our meeting, Edward?'

'Of course,' Edward replied, without hesitation. 'But I do not think it would be right, or fair, for all of you to challenge him in the hall. He has been expecting this. He is quite frail. Why don't some of you come with me and see him at his residence? That would be less threatening. What do you say?' Edward put a forkful of food in his mouth, as he waited through a brief silence for a response.

Mr Workman replied: 'Myself, Mrs Edmunds, Joe and anyone else who wants to come then – if the room agrees. Edward?' Waiting for a reply, Mr Workman's authoritative tone hung belligerently in anticipation.

A pause (with chewing). 'Okay,' Edward replied. This basic food made him feel sick, but he was hungry and thin. He could not afford to turn it down, based on it not tasting nice. All they had was the vegetable patch and a small number of livestock. All the food, rationed out carefully to feed these good people. Edward took his time eating, to give the Governor time to get up. He was a late riser.

The meeting started soon afterwards, as people gathered at the stage-end of the hall. Some people went off out or upstairs, uninterested in what was happening. Most stayed to hear the exchange of views.

'Should we gather ourselves and the few possessions we have, and leave?' suggested Mr Workman.

The crowd murmured a small noise in support, rather weakly. Edward realised that they had no great resolve to shout in support. He watched closely. He knew that Mr Workman and Mrs Edmunds had been trying to rallying support for a while. He knew that they were good at it, though the amount of resistance recorded here would not reflect whether the Governor was to be ousted. It would reflect that it didn't matter whether he was there or not. He wasn't any more likely to move that cloud on (the real cause of their pain) than any other member of the town.

'Should we ask Governor Westbrook to stand down?' Mr Workman asked directly. Silence this time. He didn't seem to have convinced himself that a change of leadership would make a difference.

'A good sign,' Edward thought.

Mr Workman stood silently, waiting and looking expectantly across the room. 'Or should we stay here and just wait to die? Not even the nomads and raiders come anymore.'

'Coincidence,' Edward thought, having recalled his conversation with the Governor, just yesterday, on the lack of nomad beggars and thieves to their town.

'Do we have good cause to overturn our Governor and replace him?' He pushed for an answer.

'No,' the crowd mumbled dismissively, finally raising energy enough to throw this option into the long grass. The people gathered there had rejected the rebellion. It was clearly going against the troublemakers. Edward smiled resiliently. This was the point where he would decide whether to return to the Governor and give him the rundown, before they came to talk to him. Hoping he wouldn't be spotted, he rose off his chair, turned to creep out, to give the Governor good news of their continuing support, but as he did his name was called by the speaker, surprising him. Edward winced, and turned to face him.

'Edward!' he yelled again from the platform, filling the room with his voice. Everyone looked round. 'Where are you going?' Mr Workman was a popular elder, with all his wits about him, despite his age. Nothing got past him. Not even Edward. 'Would you like to tell the Governor that we need to discuss some possible courses of action?'

Edward smiled at Mr Workman. Support for the Governor

was as good as support for him. He straightened himself up and took a moment, scratching his face and then said, 'Yes. Of course, Mr Workman.' Edward turned to walk out of the building, to show a little defiance towards him.

'Wait a minute, young man.' Mr Workman, again commanding the room, went on: 'What do you plan to say? Shall we all go? After all, we are almost the entire population of Goscote.' He swept his hand across the room, as if to imply that all the people there agreed to go and harass the poor man. Edward knew that most did not.

'No, sir. Please, just a few go and see the Governor. I'm sure if all of us go, we'd overwhelm the man.' Edward now wanted a proper cue to leave without being summoned back, looking directly at Mr Workman while he waited.

'Don't grin at me, Edward.' Edward wasn't sure he was grinning. 'I was twice the man you were at your age,' Mr Workman scolded him. Edward knew he couldn't see far enough to know whether he was 'grinning' or not. He didn't retaliate. 'Just a few volunteers then, please,' Mr Workman instructed the room, conceding Edward's request.

'Okay, let's go. The Governor is in.' As Edward led the delegation, they stood up and headed towards the double doors. The others rising and moving in different directions, some staying to chat with their friends and relatives. The delegation took a minute or two to make their way to the doors, across the large hall and out into the street. They chatted and walked the couple of hundred yards to Governor Westbrook's house. As they walked, a loud boom echoed up the street. Not as loud as a bomb or explosion, but loud enough to stop the crowd from chatting. They walked more slowly, unsure what it was. Unsure whether to stand still and listen. The noise echoed against the empty buildings. They stopped walking to look around, puzzled. It was more a crumbling sound, difficult to decode. Edward strained his ears to listen if there was any other noise to locate the first one. It became quiet. They looked at each other, shrugged and then continued to walk. Edward felt something was wrong. They arrived outside and he climbed the five steps up to the door, to speak, before they all had a chance to clamber in and startle the Governor.

'Perhaps we should speak to him down here. I'll run upstairs and ask him to come down.' Edward waited for a sign of approval. A nod and a smile or two supported his suggestion, before he moved inside, through the hall and up the stairs.

He imagined the Governor watching from the window, thinking that this might be an angry mob. He strode three stairs at a time for the next couple of flights, then one at a time for the last flight. He turned the last corner into the open door of the apartment, puffing as he ran out of breath. As he walked in, he saw dust in the air. He felt his gut tighten with anxiety.

'Governor?' He spoke into the air, listening and expecting a prompt answer. The sound of his voice seemed muffled as if it had bumped into the heavy cloud of dust in the room and just stopped there for a second before dying aimlessly. No sound came back. No Governor's voice replying to his question. Just an eerie empty silence. He paused for a second or two, knowing what might appear as he edged into the apartment. Walking slowly across the apartment, he arrived at the door of the bathroom and there was the Governor, under a small pile of rubble, blood dripping from him, seeping into the dust, which had settled on the side of the bath. The Governor was dead. The ceiling had fallen in. Edward looked up at the hole to see if there had been any foul play, but this building was falling apart, just like all the others in Goscote. Edward was in no position to judge, but knowing the circumstances, and the people he shared his life with, there would be no foul play. He was dead and there were no signs to show that there was any third party involved. It was very obviously an accident.

Edward just looked for a minute, transfixed by this dead man he could hardly see, beneath the lumps of concrete and plaster. Feeling suddenly squeamish, the sight of the injuries sent a shiver of raw nervous energy through his skin. He shook it off and looked away. He stared down at the floor, leant against the wall, unable to look, his emotions welling up inside. He had to get a grip of himself. Tears came into his eyes as he fought them back, screwing his face up into a knot as he tried, his fist tightly clenched against his head. He slowly straightened up, then pushed and rubbed his hands over his face, trying to massage away the pain. Hoping to distract it from his mind to something physical. He'd have to go and tell them. They'd be waiting. Eventually he edged back towards the door, turning slightly, wondering whether another minute would be all right. Whether he should say a prayer or just go over and hold the Governor's hand and say goodbye. But he didn't. He just paused and looked at him.

It was another death. The Governor had been like a father to Edward. Nowhere near as comforting and authoritarian as his own father, but close enough. As close to him as he wanted, or needed. He went back downstairs to tell the people that their leader was dead.

He walked step by step down the stairs, his footfalls getting louder as the people chatted. Edward listened to the echoing sound his footsteps made through the stairwell. He didn't know why, but the sound made him feel better, thinking they might be more placid and kind if they thought an angry man was coming down the stairs to see them. A flicker of a smile passed, turning to an angry grimace, his mind fizzing with mixed emotions. Small idiosyncratic signs of emotional distress that he would try to hide once he'd arrived downstairs. One more dead friend or relative to miss and to ache for.

When he got there, he appeared at the door briefly inviting Mr Workman in on his own, asking him for a word. The crowd started groaning under their breath. Mr Workman stepped in. He looked behind him towards Mrs Edmunds who was shrugging in disapproval. He closed the door behind him, as the people waited. Edward, quietly, told Mr Workman what had happened.

'The crash we heard?'

Edward nodded. 'The ceiling fell in, by the looks of it.' Tears welling in his eyes, he looked at the floor and back up. He felt like smashing Mr Workman in the face, quickly thinking about what the fallout would be. How he'd be thrown off the community and banished, though Joe would try to stand up for him. Mr Workman going into shock for a few days, saying he didn't know why Edward would do such a thing to a frail old man. He tempted himself with ultimate failure, shame and personal disaster. Played with the idea of throwing it all in the air and seeing his fragile life come tumbling out of the sky in pieces. He would have to leave this catastrophe of a town behind. That was something he couldn't do. He rubbed the tears out of his eyes again.

'I'll tell them.' Mr Workman turned away, Edward hoping he hadn't noticed what had just gone through his head. Mr Workman opened the door and broke the news to the others. Edward focused his gaze on the green paint flaking off the inside of the door.

'I'm afraid Governor Westbrook has had an accident,' Mr Workman said. 'It appears this wretched building has collapsed on the top floor and has landed on him.'

Edward watched the back of his head, listening to his words as they echoed through the open door to the waiting people. His eyes filled with tears again, as he looked round to see the reaction. One or two of the women began to cry, covering their faces with their hands and running off back to the safety of the hall. The men looked down, trying not to show their emotions too much, looking off to their womenfolk as they ran. A real blow, after everything they'd been through.

'This really is the last straw,' Mr Workman mumbled to himself and to God. To the men standing in front of him.

'Where's Edward?' one of the elderly women asked.

Edward, hearing this, popped out from behind the door, and immediately saw Mrs Edmunds standing in front of him. 'Why are you hiding? Come out and explain yourself,' she said, angrily. Edward moved from behind the door.

'Now, now, Mrs Edmunds. This is as much a loss to Edward as to any of us.' Mr Workman saw her contempt for Edward and headed it off. The peacemaker as usual between the stalwart and upstart.

'He's so smug, Mr Workman,' Mrs Edmund said, with her arms tightly crossed, her pink and blue woollen cardigan crumpled round the folds in her arms. Although she looked motherly, she was far from it.

Edward was devastated. Dropping his guard, he glared at her, letting her see how hurt he was. Mrs Edmunds noticed his reaction and stopped, but stared at him, dropping her arms to her side in remission. She backed off, calmed down and turned to walk home. He stood, leant up against the frame of the door, as if he would collapse if it wasn't there to hold him. He stayed silent while one by one everyone left to go back to the hall, except Mr Workman. They slowly walked away in silence. It seemed to him like a statement, but it wasn't. That was the direction in which they needed to go. But by God it felt like they were showing him their backs. No one seemed to have much sympathy. They did, but like Edward they had no strength to offer something they were barely able to give themselves. Everyone felt numb with pain.

He wasn't sure what to do about this sudden event. Mr Workman put his hand on Edward's arm, and let it gently slide back off. He smiled and walked off to catch up with the others. Edward had to retreat to the tower block and his telescope. This was his zone of comfort. On the way, he thought he might stay there for a few weeks. Just staring into space maybe, until the worried community came to find him. When they arrive, he'd refuse to speak to them. Perhaps he would become a sage. Some silent monastic protest to frighten them, to punish them for their moaning, complaining middle-class rebellion against the Governor.

He arrived back, looking up at the building as he approached. It had uneventful, lonely, crumbling architecture, but Edward knew this was the only building with a clear view of the sky, above the other roofs. He walked in as the doors swung shut behind him and climbed the stairs. The Governor's body remained where it was for the time being, no one having the heart to move him. Tomorrow he'd have to gather enough emotional and physical strength to do so himself, but right now he sought some sanctuary in his hideout. Time to think about what he was going to do and finally form the plan he so desperately searched for.

CHAPTER THREE

Edward arrived prepared to move the Governor's body for burial, remove the rubble, clean the body, and move him back downstairs. He paused again at the door for a moment, feeling emotionally exhausted, having thought about what he had done, leaving him there as if he didn't care about the man. There were no funeral directors or morticians to sort this out. He loved the man. He didn't want this responsibility, but it fell to him nevertheless. He took in a long breath before opening the door. He walked in and stopped at the other side of the door, closing it behind him. He walked through the room, every movement feeling slow and laboured, forcing himself to take each step, bracing himself for the Governor's body again. But it had already been done.

'Mr Workman, no doubt,' Edward said out loud. His head dropped with relief, his legs trembling with adrenalin. He stared into the room, at the bath. The dust still covering everything, except large patches where the blood-soaked dust had been. Now he would just get on with his life.

He would not show emotion here. He would just carry on, death losing its sting. Knowing that it was a part of life. He turned and walked to the desk, fingering through the few papers the Governor kept. He skirted the desk, eventually sitting in the chair, leaning forward and resting his head in his hands. Conceivably this was the point he would have begun sobbing uncontrollably. He thought about what a relief it would be, but the emotions just weren't there. What a luxury it would be. All the repressed grief and pain had deadened his nerves. Life was going to continue. This was no pain – to lose the Governor. Just another day; concerned by his lack of emotion, but perhaps unable to relive the grieving process for the fourth time.

He stood, and taking nothing from the Governor's desk went to the Town Hall to find out what was happening. There was nothing of importance to do there, just like the job itself. A self-sustaining community doesn't need a governor. They just have one because most of the people felt they wanted one. Edward was sure if he actually asked, they wouldn't have any specific reason why they needed a new governor.

As he arrived, he spotted Madeline. Could he avoid her without upsetting her? He didn't want her to know his state of mind. He didn't want her to think that if she or Simon died, he wouldn't grieve. If he showed no emotion now, would Madeline suspect he had become cold? She walked over to him. He could see she was nervous and self-conscious. He had no choice now. To relieve her he sped up slightly and suddenly she was there. As they went to embrace, he jumped with the sudden physical presence of her, lifting him quickly from his thinking, his trance.

'How are you feeling, Edward?'

To his relief, he saw immediately that she understood. Something unspoken between them. Something only people who are close could understand. Just a look and a feeling, saying it all.

'Okay. Mr Workman's a good man. He cleaned up Ken, and moved the rubble for me. I was sure I'd have to do it today.'

'I asked him to, but he beat me to it. He'd already started,' she said, looking underneath his bowed head to catch his eyes and read the emotion in them.

He wondered if she had helped to clear up the blood. Tears began to well up in Edward's eyes, but he ordered them away. He refused to let go of his emotions. He needed to be cold. Emotions would interfere with survival.

They hugged some more as Mr Workman walked over to them to offer condolences and explain himself. There was a section in the hall cordoned off for the dozen or so children to play. As Edward talked with Mr Workman, he could see a child waving at him. It was Simon. Edward waved back. The conversation faded in and out, as he tried to get his bearings. Mr Workman talked continually, while Edward scanned for his close friends; reassuring himself, having seen his family, he needed to complete the set. He tested them to see if he could see all of his key friends and relatives right from this spot. From this he would determine who was going to be there for him, now and in the future. Through the kitchen door, he could see the vegetable patch; the door flung open as wide as it could go. The livestock and garden were just where he could see his friend Joe, kneeling over his pregnant dog, Molly. No doubt he would speak to Joe soon. That dog could provide some puppies for the community. She had a great deal of responsibility; the male dog had long gone, so it was now or never. Edward made a mental note to go and speak with Joe as soon as possible. He could see Joe's wife leaning over the vegetables, pulling weeds and turning over soil with a trowel. Her skirt blowing in the breeze.

Right now, his focus came back to Mr Workman as he explained to Edward about the funeral arrangements. Edward listened and nodded politely as he discussed readings from the Bible. Naturally, he was asked to give a speech about the Governor.

'We'll be as traditional as possible. A few readings and quite a lot of us want to say some words about him. You'll join them I hope?'

'Yes,' Edward replied, as he strung together keywords from the conversation, snapping back into proper concentration. Mr Workman pulled a face, but said nothing.

'I admired the Governor, Edward, as much as I criticised him.' Mr Workman paused for a second, checking he was being listened to. 'He was a good man. I'm sorry for your loss.' Mr Workman looked devastated, as he ended the conversation.

'I understand. Thank you, for what you did. I'm not sure I would have had the strength this time.'

'I know.' Mr Workman patted him on the arm and walked away.

The funeral was held that afternoon. As the people gathered, Edward explained their history. How he became his counsellor, his father leaving him at such a young age, responsibility landing upon him unexpectedly. Edward explained to the gathering how his father was Counsel to three Governors, and although never selected for governorship himself, his father saw his place as vital to the administration. Shortly after Governor Ken Westbrook took over, his father died. It was then that Ken decided to take on his eldest brother, bypassing an election. It had been some years since an election had taken place. Counsel to the Governor had taken on the same characteristics as a deputy. Ken was the son of a senior politician in the county government, back before Goscote, other towns and nations fell foul of these hard times. They had all seen so much tragedy in these years.

Edward then began to tell them of his brother. 'My brother passed away less than two years ago. I would now be alone if it wasn't for Madeline and Simon.' He looked over at them, as Madeline struggled to hold Simon still, squirming around as young kids do. 'The Governor and I were as good as family. We trusted each other. It is such a shame that he died in a way such as this. I will miss him.'

Edward walked off the stage silently, as people wept. He felt guilty again, this time that the speech wasn't long enough, not passionate enough.

Mr Workman stood and read from the Bible. Each member of the community, who had wanted to speak, climbed the stage and added personal stories and tributes. Edward slipped into his subconscious, not listening to the words. He sat silently, his mind clear and emptied of troubling thoughts and feelings, numb to the great losses he and others had suffered. He wished the Governor had survived, another ten years, twenty years. Maybe more. He did not want to take his role, so empty and pointless. Edward had no idea how he was going to save his people from this extinction. He was no Governor. Just a lost soul.

Soon after the funeral, he walked back to the tower block once more, and looked at that cloud again, through his telescope. He watched for a time, wondering whether the voice he had heard had meant anything at all. As he watched, he saw another cloud of dust form into a separate clump as it fell away from the huge mass above it. But as he watched, it didn't do what he expected. The clump was no clump. It slowly formed into a funnel. It twisted as the tip dropped towards Earth, the white and orange mass entwining itself, like a tornado. The fluffy vapour coming to the top and then folding underneath before another came and went majestically. Then a second funnel grabbed his attention from the corner of the telescope's view. And a third. They then died away one by one, disappointment coming and going just like the tease of an event that signalled change turning out to be nothing after all. He'd seen these before, just once or twice. A rare highlight. Perhaps it was a sign from the Governor that he had reached heaven?

CHAPTER FOUR

Edward sat for some time, wondering whether this was the event he was supposed to be looking out for. A certain amount of scepticism had crept in over the years. He'd never been tempted to believe that he would create or witness a sudden miraculous revival. The funnels disappeared and nothing else happened. He sank into a depression, and just watched for another hour on and off, looking at the sky, scanning, looking for anything that the little voice had alluded too. He was so glad he'd had the insight to listen to Mr Taylor. The small voice never made a promise or a prediction. Just a polite suggestion. But it stayed in his mind, sometimes to the point of obsession, keeping himself vigilant to change.

Disappointed, he gave up and dropped the telescope down to its rest position. In one last glance he noticed one man walking slowly up Broad Street, the orange light picking him out against the silvery glow from the frost that covered the silent, empty street. He was a strong-looking man, with a cloak, and covering his shoulders was a flap of material, presumably to keep off the rain. If he was heading for the Town Hall, he was heading in the wrong direction. Edward thought for a second, running through the possible events that might have brought him here. He bounded down the stairs, into the street to meet this man before he disappeared. As he reached the ground floor, he flung the door open, catching his own momentum with his hand on the doorframe. The man was standing right in front of him, both of them startled by each other. A moment of silence passed, while they figured out whether they were friend or foe. Edward spoke.

'Who are you?' he asked with suspicion.

'I have come to help you,' he replied, quickly and lightly. The man was in his fifties and balding.

'Help?' Edward said, not knowing exactly what he should say. He was puzzled somewhat by this offer, as if the idea had popped into the stranger's head just to explain away Edward's suspicions.

'Yes. I have come to help you survive this bad time. I travel a lot, speaking to people about how to survive. Try and keep things going, until the cloud clears.' He pattered off the words like a salesman, as if he'd said them a thousand times.

'Oh!' Edward brightened up. Perhaps he was from central government, he thought. 'We only have about a hundred or so people left alive. We could die out pretty soon. It's quite possible.'

'Yes, well, I can help you. Where is everyone?'

'In the hall. I'll show you. Are you from central government? Are we beginning to recover?' Edward asked, looking back as they walked.

'I don't know about that. But I can help you to get through this.'

'What is your name?'

'Dean. What's yours?'

'Edward. I'm Counsel to the Governor.'

'Right, I'll have to meet him.'

Edward stayed silent. He didn't tell him about his death, for fear he'd know that the town currently had no governor. Besides, the alarm bells were ringing. Was this guy for real or not? They walked towards the hall, cutting nervously through the alley, not quite trusting each other. Edward noticed a slight shiver in him. Was it the cold or was he nervous? They walked in between two buses, parked next to each other, and Dean looked with interest at them as the Town Hall came into sight. Edward watched everything he did, looking away when he did. He was almost unable to take his eyes off him.

As they walked in, the stranger looked the place up and down, putting his hands on his hips. There were a few people in beds in the hall, one or two moving about upstairs. The lights were off in the hall and a dim light gave the place a magical feel.

'It's late, so I'll find you a bed. You can stay down here until the morning. I'll introduce you then.'

Dean agreed, and was shown to a bed. Edward took up a bed nearby and that night slept little, wondering who this man was. There was a fascination about him. The voice he heard. He dared not think this was it. The turn of events, the Governor dying, the funnels of cloud he'd seen. He lay awake staring at the walls and the ceiling of the hall, listening to every movement, wanting daybreak to come. He thought about all the possibilities. If he had not been looking through the telescope, would Dean have passed through, thinking that the town was deserted? It was quite possible.

Morning came and activity began early. The early risers soon realised there was a stranger sleeping in the hall and silently raised the alarm, as the younger, fitter men found a weapon, and Mr Workman prepared to stir Dean to find out who he was. They discussed things first in the kitchen, and then Mr Workman, Joe and two of the others volunteered to walk over and give him a nudge with a stick. They opened the backdoor, reached around the side and grabbed the sticks leant up against the outside wall, there for such occasions as this. Suddenly Edward arrived.

'Mr Workman!' he yelled across the hall, waking Dean who sat up and wiped his eyes, trying desperately to focus. The three large men and Mr Workman stared at him, armed with their sticks. He rose up from the floor, and stood straight, with some effort to face them, looking worried.

'This is Dean, everyone,' Edward proclaimed breathlessly, as he hurried across the floor. 'He arrived last night. He's from central government.'

'Oh... .' Dean tried to deny this, but it was too late.

'Welcome, Dean. Perhaps you could tell us what has been happening for these last few years. Are we all going to die?' Joe asked him in a matter-of-fact way that startled him.

'Well, I don't think you're going to die. I have a few things to teach you so that you don't. I have travelled quite a bit, doing this; teaching people survival techniques. No doubt you have a lot of questions.'

'You're bloody right we have questions,' Joe said.

'Joe, don't be hostile. He could be handy. He could save our lives,' Edward exclaimed, holding an arm across him, to keep him from getting any closer.

'Yes,' Dean replied nervously. Still dressed in his wax coat, Dean stretched a little, and asked for food. The women and children began to come in to admire this strange visitor. With much of the community now standing in front of Dean, staring at him, Edward turned and addressed them.

'This is Dean,' he bowed slightly, 'and he is from central government.' A noise of delight and interest murmured across the hall, echoing slightly. 'He has come to teach us a few survival techniques. Hopefully, this is the answer to our prayer.' He stood aside. 'Dean.'

'Yes. Hi. I am sure everyone wants to know what is happening out there in the wider world, and I have to say I know little. What I do know is something about how I am able to help see you through this difficult period. I will teach you to increase crop yields in the low sunlight during the months when the cloud,' he looked up, 'is above us. I will also try to prepare you to develop your technologies and increase your activities so that you can begin to thrive, rather than just survive. You are barely surviving right now. I have done plenty of work like this in the past and it will take a matter of weeks to get things moving in the right direction.' He looked to Edward to round off.

The people were happy with Dean's arrival and introduction. They began to get ready to prepare food for breakfast and get organised for the day ahead. He had sent a good vibe, reverberating throughout those gathered around him.

'A good start,' he said quietly to Edward, 'judging by the reaction here.'

'Thank you, Dean.' Edward turned to him and gripped his arm as Mr Workman glared at them both with distrust. Dean and Edward had already begun to forge an alliance. They had clearly clicked, and Mr Workman seemed unsure as to where this man had come from. He immediately went to find Mrs Edmunds, a reliable source of dissent. Something was up.

Edward quietly noted Mr Workman's reaction. He would have to think how he was going to counter any protest before it began.

Dean and Edward spent the day talking through all kinds of things. Dean had to steer the conversation away from talk of central government, which wasn't difficult, as he had set himself up as someone who was out of contact with the mainstream power for most of the time. They talked through increasing energy production, increasing crop yields, and livestock husbandry. They discussed the Governor and his unfortunate death. When they arrived back at the hall for the evening meal, people gathered to speak to Dean, to ask him questions. Mr Workman stayed back throughout the session. But Edward noted him looking intensely and regularly at him, while he helped to organise the tables and chairs.

Come 5.30, May, Joe's wife, ran in screaming. 'They've arrived! They've arrived!'

Startled by her reaction, everyone stood up and went over, pushing past her into the backyard, where she had come from. Edward and Dean picked a stick each, and marched out with many of the other men. May was nearly hysterical, with tears rolling down her cheeks. As they arrived, the crowd parted to let Edward and Dean through. Molly, the sheepdog, had given birth to five healthy puppies. This was at least the fourth time she had tried, the puppies arriving stillborn or dying young. These puppies were strong, and alive, wriggling around, with the afterbirth still on the floor. It was the second good thing to have happened to them this year, including contact with Dean. The spirit of the place improved just a bit, with smiles and lively discussions going on around Edward as he stroked Molly. She looked up with a half-exhausted, half-relieved loving look in her eye, unsure what the fuss was about, unable to understand how much it meant to them for her to have done this simple, but marvellous thing.

Next to kneel down over them was Joe, scooping up one puppy in his hand, to look at him and then returning him, taking up the next one, checking for any conspicuous problems. The crowd moved slowly back into the hall, careful not to startle Molly any more, while she began a delicate recovery. Dean, Edward and Joe – Molly's owner – stayed and watched for a while. Dean was offered a puppy of his own. He accepted, smiling and nodding.

'You'll have to wait a while until the puppies are ready to leave their mother,' Joe explained, as he looked back down at them looking pleased.

Having already been promised one, Edward chose his dog, a male.

Joe looked up at Edward. 'What you going to call him?'

'Taylor.'

'After old Mr Taylor, the teacher?' he asked.

'Not really,' Edward lied, distancing himself from discussion about Mr Taylor.

'What about yours, Dean? Do you want a male or female?' Joe asked.

'I'll have a male and I'll call him Evan.'

'That's nice,' May said. Joe smiled. He felt sure that he was here for the right reasons.

They moved back into the hall, eventually leaving Joe and May to attend to the dogs. The town went about their business, many of them staying to spend time with Dean. He was being warmly welcomed by all. Even Mr Workman, still with a touch of distrust, saw how happy the people were around him. Things were looking up at last.

CHAPTER FIVE

At first light everyone organised themselves for the day's chores, each person able and active heading off for different parts of the community. Edward, Dean, Mr Workman and Joe decided to dedicate the day to organising the power supplies. The power was limited, and most of the community had to be in bed early, to preserve the energy for more important things. The generator was located in the basement of the hall, and was the original emergency generator, now used as the primary source of power. The four men went down to inspect the job. Dean studied the top and clambered down onto his knees, to inspect the underside, and then crawled round to the back, almost disappearing underneath, while the others looked at each other, not sure what Dean had in mind. He then noticed a second redundant generator, and looking back and forth at both, he thought for a while.

'One engine could run much of the needs of the community, while the other can be converted to take organic material.' Dean's voice was muffled by the giant machine.

Surprised and sceptical, they looked at each other. They questioned whether any of them had the technical skill.

'That's pretty sophisticated technology for us. I'm not sure we'd have the right skills or parts,' Mr Workman explained. But Dean challenged them.

'Oh, don't worry, Mr Workman. I have the technical skill and all you need to do is find a few pieces of kit from the town.' He got back on his feet and around the other side. 'The first job is to remove the engines from the two old buses parked outside the hall,' he said, pointing towards them, as if they were in sight from where they stood. 'Joe and Edward, do you want to volunteer?'

'Of course,' Edward replied. They climbed the stairs and disappeared through the low door, dipping their heads.

'We'll need wiring. Is there a good supply of wire nearby?' Dean asked from the back of the generator.

'Oh yes, there's quite a lot of it in the basement of that old tower block. It was originally stripped of its wiring, during an unfinished project when the community was larger. Much of it was taken down to the basement for storage and stayed there.'

'What kind of wiring?'

'All kinds.'

'Okay. Perhaps I could take a look.'

'Of course, Dean. Follow me.'

Dean had moved underneath the second generator as he spoke to Mr Workman. He slowly got up, his bones creaking and clicking from his kneeling position, brushing off the dust. They walked up the stairs, back through an access hatch, around the side of the hall, across the street and back down through the alley to the tower. They climbed down into another basement, and fumbled through the darkness.

'You know what we've done, don't you, Dean?'

'Forgotten a lamp?'

'Yes. I'll fetch one from the hall. I'll be back in a minute.'

Mr Workman went back up the stairs and Dean slowly followed. He could just see the mass of wires up to the ceiling in the dim light. He looked a while and then climbed the stairs and then onto the next level, onto the first floor. The dust covering the basement stairs was thick, and he immediately noticed that there was no dust on the stairs up to the first floor, nor the second, as he climbed. He had seen Edward come out of here when he first arrived. As he reached each floor, he went through the door poking his head around into the large office spaces. When he reached the fifth he saw a few things on the far left, down one of the long side rooms. He walked through and found Edward's things lying around. A notepad and pencil, the telescope, the screen and the bed. There were a few other small things lying around. He was puzzled. He went back downstairs, and said nothing to Mr Workman about it. He just gave him a friendly smile and got on with things.

As Mr Workman arrived back, Dean was sitting on the

bottom stair. He stood up, turning back down into the basement. Dean soon found what he wanted, as they filled up a box or two to take back.

'You've lived here all your life, then, Mr Workman?' asked Dean.

'Yes. More or less.'

'They're good people. This is one of the nicest of the communities I've visited. Strangers aren't always welcome,' Dean told him.

'I think it must be charisma that got you accepted so quickly. And the fact that the gypsies and raiders don't come anymore. They probably pass us by. We had an illness some years ago, took most of the population, including my father and his sister, my aunty.'

'Really? I'm sorry to hear that.'

'Long time ago.' Mr Workman cracked a smile.

They passed Edward and Joe as they lifted the heavy bonnet from the bus. Dean stopped.

'We've got to get that engine unhooked before nightfall!'

Edward and Joe looked at each other in disbelief as Dean smiled.

Edward had noted that Mr Workman and Dean had come from the tower's basement, judging from the boxes they each carried. He studied them both, as they passed, including the boxes with red and grey leads spilling over the edges. He was worried his hideout had been discovered. Nobody went to that side of Broad Street, or the tower. Mostly the allotment, and at one time the Governor's residence, a hundred yards further down Broad Street. He would have to move his things upstairs a flight and cover it up. He hadn't been too concerned, but he knew instantly that Dean was sharper than most. It wouldn't take long to discover, if he had taken the time to look upstairs. Concerned, Edward was anxious to work quickly. He would have to stay there tonight. How was he going to slip away from Dean?

The people were curious. They wanted to hear everything Dean had to say. Edward approached Madeline first, telling her he'd see her in the morning first thing. She looked at him in dismay. She stayed silent, though Edward thought perhaps an argument was brewing. He left before she started. He'd have to spend more time at home, or bring her over to the tower. Next he informed Dean he would not be around for the rest the evening and slipped away as soon as he got the chance.

Dean enthralled his audience, with his stories of wondrous building projects undertaken by other governments, and the new way of life springing up all over the world. While this was happening, Edward quietly moved his things up to the top floor. It would be an early night. It was never complete darkness during daylight, when the cloud was overhead. But it was dark enough to make life very difficult for all of them, especially when it snowed. That was really tough. Edward always dreaded waking up to it. It was always hard on the old and weak. It was also hard on the kids. They got so cold that mothers, though there were only a few, would have to climb into bed with them for most of the night to keep them from freezing to death. All this, with nothing either Edward or the Governor could do to help.

Once people began to move up to their rooms and apartments, Dean focused his attention on going back to the tower to find Edward. Dean had focused a great deal of his attention on him right from the start, as if Edward was essential to this town's survival.

He arrived at the fifth floor soon after ten o'clock, and quietly moved up into the long room Edward had chosen. Dean still did not know what exactly went on up here. When he arrived the things had gone. He went back out, guessing that he would have moved to the top floor, and hoping he hadn't moved buildings. Sure enough he found Edward on the seventh floor. He walked in and made Edward almost leap in fright.

'Edward. Thought I'd find you here.'

Edward grinned in embarrassment at having jumped at Dean's sudden arrival. 'It's not a great secret. It's just my way of getting through the day. A place to think through our predicament and try and come up with something,' Edward explained, ending his sentence by looking briefly at the floor, as if guilty of some petty, dirty crime.

'Does Madeline know?'

'I don't know that she does. She might have guessed where I go by now. It doesn't matter anyway. It's hardly grounds for divorce. Mind you, she's getting fed up with me staying away, so I'll have to cut down. I'm not sure I want anyone to know, not even her.'

'Why keep it a secret?' Dean asked.

'Because there were times when people tried to figure a way to get over these problems. Move the cloud on. They were hailed as heroes and when their plans failed, they were seen as charlatans. In the end, people stopped trying, didn't they? You should know that.' He suddenly realised he was talking to someone who would know as well as he did.

Edward saw a flicker of pain in Dean. The source of which was unidentified as yet. The same feeling of distrust returned. Edward took note and cleared his mind, moving on to another subject. 'Dean, tell me about these buildings. I missed most of it.'

'You tell me what you can see through that telescope and I'll tell you what you want to know.'

Edward sat on his bed on the floor, and Dean on the cold plastic floor tiles. Edward told him about the voice he heard and the day Dean arrived, how he'd seen the funnels, dropping from the cloud. Dean nodded with interest without commenting. Then Dean explained that the buildings were not built. Puzzled, Edward suspected a problem, a lie. If he was lying, why was he explaining it to him?

Dean said he simply had no clue whether the buildings had been built or not. They were super cities, built holistic communities, with state-of-the-art technologies, flood and earthquake defences, and legions of gadgets and labour-saving devices. Happy, well people, and healthy democratic governments. Edward was confused. Dean explained to him that the last he heard, this is what other governments had done. Britain had not, as far as he knew.

'But this is not what you have told my people down in the hall, is it?'

'Your people? It's good to hear you call them "your people",' Dean replied. 'No, I lied. I want them to believe in themselves, Edward. I want them to believe that their government is working hard and to be motivated and optimistic. Believe me it makes a massive difference to survival.'

'Well, if I was to trust you on this one, then at least I know we will benefit. I presume this is our secret?' he asked.

'Just as your telescope is?' Dean replied.

Edward agreed. An alliance was formed between them that night.

'Please keep this den of mine quiet for now. I decided I would keep it like that, either until I had a plan or until someone found it. Oh, and please don't come here uninvited. Please be courteous and wait for an invite. This is how I survive. How I remain sane and happy. In all my thinking about how to help, the only thing I managed to come up with was being optimistic and happy. Keep people feeling happy and they'll do a little extra when times are hard. I came up with my one idea right here; well, down two flights anyway.' An awkward pause. 'I'm kind of glad you inspired me to move up here,' he said, looking around. 'The view is a lot better than I presumed. I didn't think a floor or two would make much difference, but it definitely has.'

'Do you mind if I take a look through your telescope?' Dean asked.

Edward hesitated then agreed. 'Sure'.

Dean later returned to the hall, and crept back in. Tomorrow, the engines were going to be moved, and everyone would be needed.

Edward sat thinking through each piece of the day. Feeling optimistic was new to him, but Dean bothered him. He was genuine and mysterious. Edward sat on the floor shivering, still working through the issues he cared about. His arms were tightly curled around himself, his chin resting into his thick woollen pullover. He thought of Madeline and Simon; how he'd become more emotionally distant from them this last year. Not sure how to move on, and keep her happy. His father was emotionally distant, and Edward guessed perhaps his grandfather as well. Promising himself he would not be like that, but finding he had little choice. Unable to break down the paper-thin barrier that stopped him from communicating with Madeline in the way he really wanted to. Paper-thin, but strong enough he couldn't break through. Feeling imprisoned by it. He ended this thinking time by imagining the future now that Dean was helping them. But no matter how hard he tried, he couldn't think beyond hardship. The easy life well outside his grasp, the future still uncertain.

The community buzzed for days during and after the refit of the generators, and Dean's stories. Everyone was motivated, happy and hopeful. One time, Dean turned up after a morning walk, with a box full of earthworms. This would help increase crop yields, keeping the soil well turned and filled with nutrients. No one had a clue where he'd found them and no one asked. He appeared one afternoon, walking along Broad Street, right in the middle of the road, as Joe and Mr Workman were working on the new light fittings they'd rescued from a suburban school. A big grin on Dean's face, a box held up to his chin. Joe climbed down from the ladder to greet him, and they peered into the box. Dean looked up and said, 'Worms.'

'No kidding,' Joe replied.

'We'll put them in the allotment.'

Dean passed them to Edward and then clapped his hands to remove the pieces of soil and sand. Edward carried on through the hall and kitchen to the back, and put them down on the ground. He sat down on the bench and looked across the garden. They had expanded the growing area, increased the size of the compost heap, created a better irrigation system on the larger allotment, and built a greenhouse, near to the hall, fitted with lamps to keep the plants lit, producing fruit and seed. The school they'd plundered had an amazing amount of light fittings and bulbs, which were still working. That had been another of Dean's miraculous finds. He had an amazing knack of coming across the small elements needed to do each job. If these good people weren't so rational, perhaps they would have believed a little miracle happened every day with him. Some of them did secretly believe he was a saviour. Genuinely, a man sent from God to rescue them. Many held back their feelings, but they all knew inside, and Edward noticed the warm glow in the people's faces when he was around.

'An answer to prayer,' he was told quite forthrightly, a number of times over those short months.

They had doubled their energy production, just as Dean had promised. The community was beginning to plan for the future again. He would soon be asked to stay longer and take up a post as Governor. Edward wouldn't stand in his way, he was glad of it. A chance to be Counsel to a great Governor and friend, and continue the family tradition. He would soon resume his old trusted position.

Edward was asked to request formally that Dean take up the post. Pleased to be of service, Edward went and asked, as soon as he was sure that there was general consensus, and no one would be upset or oppose the proposal. Dean was out in the allotment as Edward began to walk over to him. Several of the town's folk were standing at the kitchen door, watching as Edward climbed awkwardly over the mounds of soil, and the paths cutting through the vegetables, almost losing his balance. He looked back and grinned as he was waved on, to hurry up and ask him.

'Dean!'

He looked up as his name was called. 'Yes, Edward, what can I do for you?'

'Dean.' He clambered some more, not quite there yet. He finally settled and pulled himself together, straightening his jacket. He cleared his throat to speak. 'Er. The people, we've been talking.'

'Oh, yes.' Dean looked worried.

'We've been short of a governor since Ken Westbrook passed away. You've been very kind and very welcome. You've motivated us, and things seem different since you arrived.'

Dean lightened up as he saw where this conversation was heading.

'Would you accept an offer, if it were to be made...?' (Edward tried not to look back, aware of everyone watching him. Dean looked quickly to the side and saw them all trying to hide) '...of taking up the post of Governor?' he said clearing his throat again.

'That's very gracious of you all.' He looked over Edward's shoulder at the people at the kitchen door again, as they all suddenly looked busy. Dean smiled, returning his focus to poor Edward, slightly embarrassed. 'As we discussed, it might soon be time to move on. But, I will carefully consider this offer, Edward, and I will have an answer by tomorrow after breakfast.'

'You're going make us wait all night?'

'It would be un-gentlemanly of me to decide straightaway.'

'I suppose you're right. I'll go and tell them.'

They grinned at each other. Dean was secretly overjoyed and had more or less decided already. It was late November, halfway through the clouded months, as the days grew their darkest of the year. Dean retired that night, promising to answer their kind and gracious offer as soon as he was awake and alert the next day. Privately he had already admitted to Edward that in normal circumstances it would soon be time to move on, to help other communities, but he was getting older. Perhaps it was time to stay. He knew he should accept the offer. The townsfolk certainly hoped he would.

Chapter Six

Dean accepted the offer and was made Governor at the beginning of December, 2133. He was given the choice of living in the hall, in which there was little room left, or an apartment in Governor Westbrook's residence, which would be repaired. Careful not to risk another death, the building was checked out and to everyone's surprise Dean accepted the apartment. Many expected him not to, after the building had killed the previous Governor. But Dean was a confident engineer, and a clever man. He was sure that it would not happen again. He moved in, taking an apartment on the first floor. Edward took up his old job again as his counsel and both of them began to think about what could be done to improve general living conditions.

They discussed the look of the place, and the obvious lack of paint. 'We'll have to think of some alternative, a natural dye of some kind, to paste over the walls and clear the crumbling paintwork.'

'Plant life is no longer versatile. We'd need certain plants in large quantities to do something like that.'

'What about transport? If we were to invest some time and energy in transport we could perhaps send a mission to find other communities, see what's there,' Dean suggested.

'I'd like that. I'd go myself.'

'There's a lot that can be done. It's going to be good, Edward. This is the best time I've had in years.'

Also, Dean wondered whether new furniture could be made, as many of the townsfolk, quite used to repairing furniture, made do with what they had. There was no reason why all these things could not take place as the community grew in confidence. Dean had met someone he wanted to marry, so now a town marriage was coming up. Sheila Beckson. A forty-year-old, pretty widow, whose husband had died many years ago. She had taken a shine to Dean from the beginning. And now the town had accepted him into his natural place, a marriage would be perfect. A fairy tale. Dean and Sheila had denied rumours up until now, skilfully keeping their affair a secret. Madeline's mother had found out somehow, and Edward was feeling happy about being 'in the know'. It boosted his confidence to know what was on the minds of his people. Madeline's mother swore him to secrecy and Edward had respected Dean's privacy enough to keep it that way, instructing Madeline's mother to keep the secret a secret, if she was able.

Dean and Edward sat on the veranda in the apartment, enjoying the beginning of the summer. There was just over five weeks of warmer weather during this time. Dean didn't need Edward's approval of his wedding to Sheila, but he would seek it out nonetheless. They sat silently for a while, as Dean built up to telling him. Dean waited for a second for signs of approval or otherwise, Edward shrugging with apprehension. Dean felt it was his way of recognising his place; that Edward was and always would be the head of the community. After a brief silence, Dean told him he planned to wed Sheila. Edward smiled and congratulated him. Then they talked about the cloud; almost a what-about-the-future father-son chat, the younger man having the privilege of guiding his elder. A sign perhaps of a society falling out of its natural order.

The cloud was caught in the Earth's atmosphere, between the Earth and the Sun. Just stuck there. Not enough bulk to be blown out of the way with weapons, and big enough to disrupt society. Humanity had all but died out under its shadow.

Sheila and Dean would get married soon. Telling Edward the news was the starting gun to begin to plan the ceremony.

Edward still spent nights at the tower, looking every day, studying the cloud and the night sky. Over the last few years he had often seen a dull light behind the clouds. It was inactive, almost non-threatening. Some nights were brighter than the others and he could see it clearly and other nights he could only see a dull orange glow. He presumed it was a thicker part of the cloud, which moved ever so slightly each month, the movements carefully recorded by Edward. Eventually he remembered to ask Dean whether he knew anything about it. He invited him to come over and look. Dean might well know something that, although it might be unimportant to him, would answer these nagging questions running around in Edward's mind.

'I can see this glowing light off in the background,' Edward explained to Dean as they stood over the telescope. 'Something like a very bright planet. I could barely see it when the cloud was there in January, but since then I've seen it more clearly. It's more or less been there since Mr Taylor first let me use the telescope. I thought nothing of it at the time. I never asked him about it and I wish I had. Has central government ever studied it?'

'You could have asked me earlier,' Dean said.

'I know. It's like a puzzle, rather than something to worry about.'

'Really?' Dean said, looking up at Edward. He was slightly reserved about it, hesitating. Edward had that same feeling again. Dean was holding something back. He looked down the telescope and went quiet. Edward went for it.

'What is it, Dean?' he demanded.

'Settle down,' Dean answered, waving at him, his eye fixed to the lens.

'Well? What is it then?' Insistent, Edward pressed for a quick and truthful reply, as Dean continued to pause, feeling panicked.

'This is what the wars were over. Jupiter has a storm in the form of a giant red spot, right?'

'Yeah.'

'There was supposed to be an explosion. The storm was supposed to send all kinds of deadly chemicals and gases in a shower over the planet at any time. Astronomers were worried about it for years. The governments argued, then the cloud suddenly arrived. Where from? Nobody knew, nobody trusted each other, because producing a shield from the blast was one of the suggestions most favoured by the superpowers. When that thing arrived everyone suspected that the superpowers had done it on their own. Scientists on both sides tried to explain this wasn't the case, but the arguments continued and got worse as the impact of the cloud became apparent. This is why all the wars we fought were sporadic and confused. It wasn't the fact that someone had done it. It was that the cloud was killing off productivity and bringing on economic decline. Anyway, Jupiter never did blow, and the scientists stopped talking about it. You know the rest.'

'So there isn't going to be an explosion, and some idiot has created this cloud to shield us from something that isn't going to happen?'

'Well no, not really. It was never established where this cloud arrived from. I personally say it's just a clump of space dust that wandered in between us and the sun. It just got caught up and stayed there. But nobody knew and the conspiracy theories were rife, and the arguments raged on and on. It had no basis in fact, either the purposeful creation of the cloud, or a gas storm on Jupiter turning into an explosion.'

'What a waste…. Tragic. I didn't know any of this.'

'Well now you do,' Dean said. He walked back through the door and down the stairs, leaving Edward standing trembling from the cold, and the realisation that his world had crumbled so easily. All he had known before were consequences, not the causes of the cloud. But now he knew. His father, mother, brother and his friend Governor Westbrook, all taken away from him, were all somehow connected to the cloud. Just a cloud, causing so much misery.

The wedding arrived soon after, and Dean and Sheila were married by Mr Workman. It was supposed to be recorded by Edward in the town's records, which had been maintained, despite the chronic pen and pencil shortage. Mr Workman stood and said a few words.

'Dean has been welcomed by us all, more or less instantly into our community. He has inspired great change in us. The day after he arrived, Molly, our beloved sheepdog, successfully completes her pregnancy. Both the power supply and the agricultural yields have doubled and our lives have finally begun to take shape; hope coming back into our once dark lives. He became our Governor and Dean has now married our own Sheila and agreed to stay permanently among us. Dean, here's to you.' He held up a glass and a mixture of glasses, mugs and cups went up among the crowd to wish them a happy life.

'To Sheila and Dean!' they said.

'All that remains is to record the marriage in the diary'. Mr Workman went quiet while he shuffled around on the dais, looking under the papers on the desk and on the stand in front of him. Everyone looked puzzled, waiting for Mr Workman to finish speaking. 'All we need is a pen,' Mr Workman said finally. He looked to Edward, as Edward looked embarrassed.

'Mm. I'm not all that sure I can help you, Mr Workman,' he said looking up at him, briefly, knowing he had one pencil at the tower. This was going to be a problem. He needed to record the movements of the cloud, but he also needed to keep the tower and telescope a secret.

Edward was feeling and looking guilty. Mr Workman looked flushed with embarrassment. Silence followed, as they squirmed. Sheila looking horrified. Dean spoke up.

'It's okay. We'll record it at a later date, once we find something. Let's not spoil the day.' Dean let them off the hook, knowing Edward had one pencil at the tower. He glared across at him, not sure whether he was in trouble or not, and Edward quickly looked away. Edward would have to make it up to him immediately, before it turned bad. Even after all their happy days this last year, Edward and Dean had an unspoken mistrust. An underlying feeling, inarticulate and mysterious. Edward was going to feel tense and anxious for the next few hours. It was going to be hard to find a way to explain why his secret was apparently more important than Dean's marriage to Sheila.

The party continued with some horrible wine and a few gifts for the happy couple, and as soon as Edward had a chance he tried to head off Dean's accusations, how he had spoiled things, too mean to part with a pencil. They met just outside the backdoor to the allotment.

'You understand, Dean? I need to keep recording for all

kinds of reasons.' Edward could feel Dean was going to make this a big deal.

'Why do you keep things a secret, Edward? That's what I don't understand. It wouldn't kill you to let people know, especially your wife. This has gone on long enough, Edward. Come on.'

'I told you from the start, it was to be a secret! I suppose you've let Sheila know?'

'No. I made a promise, Edward.' Dean looked down briefly. 'Bring that pencil down tomorrow and then you can disappear it again. But I'm warning you, you need to let people know what you do up there. I cannot understand where all this is going.' Dean sounded like a leader now.

'Don't tell them, Dean.' A warning.

'Maybe someone ought to,' Dean returned the threat.

Edward filled with a sudden anger, felt like rushing him, forcing him up against the wall. Just a flash of anger, which quickly faded. They looked at each other, both looking away before parting company. Perhaps Edward wasn't happy about relinquishing governorship, now that bad feeling had edged slightly forward.

'We all have our secrets, Dean.' Edward looked him in the eye, as Dean shrank back. Where had this animosity suddenly arrived from?

Dean went pale. He walked back over to Sheila and left straightaway.

Back at the Governor's house Dean and Sheila settled down and drank and talked before going to bed. The next day they spent together, in bed, having a good time, laughing and talking, getting to know each other. Dean was keeping a secret. He was patching together his old life with the new one and trying to keep a mental note of what he'd said. In time he'd have to tell them. His secrets might be too destructive, and he was happy right now.

A week passed before Edward and Dean really spoke properly again. Dean spending time with Sheila, and Edward with Madeline and Simon. They bumped into each other in the hall of Dean's apartment. Edward had left them alone for a while, but there were issues to resolve. He took a deep breath and went to find Dean to begin work. They spoke briefly.

'Sorry, Dean, about the other night. Have you told anyone?' Edward asked.

'No,' Dean replied.

'Good.' Edward believed him. Silence followed again, the atmosphere a little tense before Dean spoke.

'I want to come and have a look at this light that you say is Jupiter,' Dean said.

'You say it's Jupiter, Dean. I don't know.'

'Whatever. Can I come up?'

'Of course you can.'

They left and walked across to the tower not saying a word. They climbed the seven floors and walked in. Dean picked up the telescope from its rest position and asked Edward for directions to find it again. Edward explained.

'This is the cloud's season, don't forget. But you'll find it through the middle, slightly to the left of the darkest patch. It lights up, an orange and yellow glow, very small.'

'Ah, yes. I see it.' As he looked, Dean spotted a funnel developing. 'A funnel?'

Edward had seen a few, but secretly keen to look in case it was a particularly large one, he anxiously waited. Dean saw it grow and grow, and spin around and down out of the cloud. Then a second funnel appeared; he remained silent.

'How big?'

'What?'

'The funnel. How big is it?' Edward asked, impatiently.

'Not big,' he lied. Dean watched a third, and then as they declined back into the cloud he passed the telescope back to Edward, clutching his pad and pencil. The funnels disappeared again, as Edward watched them go.

Dean went downstairs, and Edward told him he'd see him later. He looked again at the dying funnels, and then down at the street, not expecting to see Dean walking off in the wrong direction and disappearing into a side street. Edward quickly left the telescope and ran down the stairs to follow him.

Something was happening. What did Dean see in the telescope he'd kept quiet about?

Edward leapt down the stairs into the street, running fast to locate him as soon as possible, panicking slightly that he'd misjudged this man. That secret Dean had kept. Something mysterious, which Edward had always been aware of, was about to reveal itself. He caught him up and slowed down, hiding, trying to stay behind him, but not in view, not wanting to give himself away. Eventually after what seemed like a long walk out onto the edge of the plain, he stopped. Once in the plain he would not be able to hide. Should he confront Dean now, or wait to see what happened first? He stayed for a while, as Dean stopped, looking up into the sky, just standing still, transfixed. Edward looked up and saw nothing. He decided to catch him up. If Dean was to be trusted, he would not be startled by his sudden appearance. He walked slowly up behind him, not too quickly. As he approached, Dean looked round and spotted him.

'I thought you were there, Edward.' He was looking up.

From the sky, three objects appeared, moving at colossal speed. Dean turned his head back round, noting Edward's reaction. Edward moved back in fear, as Dean stood still, as if he knew what was coming. As they got nearer, Edward prepared to run for his life. Three large dark brown objects landed on the floor of the plain, in front of Dean, throwing up plenty of dust. Edward felt a slight shake in the ground underneath him as they landed. They were some fifty yards away and rolling towards him, the dust spewing up behind them, leaving a trail as they moved. They reached Dean, as Edward held back, and Dean moved forward as if to greet whatever they were. They rolled into position, and came to a stop, dust rising up around them and settling. Out came stands and out of one of them a hatch, with a tray and a hand-held phone or computer. Dean removed it and then spoke into it. Edward was unaware of what was actually happening, unable to see or hear the details. Dean's posture changed. Some bad news. Edward straightened up, as Dean seemed dizzy, bending down, clutching his knees to stabilise himself. He stood like that for a while, as Edward watched. The three rocks rolled off again, quickly gathering pace, and then lifting off into the air and onwards, again at massive speed, the likes of which Edward had never seen. Dean turned round and began to run towards him.

As he arrived, he grabbed Edward by the arms, and spoke to him, tears welling in his eyes. 'Edward, I have to go. I'm sorry.'

Dean began to run off back towards town. Edward ran after him.

'What's happening?' Edward shouted behind him. There was no answer. He followed Dean through the town, and instead of going straight back to the Governor's house, he turned left to go out of town along Broad Street. Edward had trouble catching him up. Somehow, this middle-aged man was able to run much faster than the younger man. After losing him, Edward quickly ran back to the tower to try and spot him. He ran back up the stairs, and grabbed the telescope, not knowing where to look. He couldn't see him. He then turned the telescope upwards to the sky to see where those strange objects had gone. As he lifted the telescope, Edward spotted what looked like stars. Right there in the sky, what seemed like a hundred thousand stars, over the horizon; over the mountains. What on Earth was happening? Edward was gripped by a sudden realisation that these lights could be an armada of aircraft, heading for Goscote. Mixed feelings swirled around his head and definite feeling of anxiety, accompanied by a pounding heart beat, which made his whole body pulse. All that waiting and suffering might be over. The voice had proved to be reliable. He couldn't believe it. The anticipation had been with him for all these years, now something was happening. He needed to decide whether to run home and tell the others or not. He looked back through the telescope and watched them come. But why were they here? Were they here to help or to make things worse?

Part Two: Goscote's Wake

CHAPTER SEVEN

As he watched, the lights grew brighter as shapes began to form into shadows of aircraft. He struggled to see what they were to start with, unsure what to think, uneasy about jumping to conclusions. Edward felt terrified. He stood back trembling, holding his hand out in front of him to see himself trembling. He went back to the window, transfixed, unable to look away. He could now see the aircraft beginning to land, jet engines throwing dust into the air around them, as they landed vertically, rocking slightly as they touched down. There was a mass of brown dust, as aircraft quickly filled the plain.

Dean was not from central government, he was running away from it. Edward finally understood all the things that had bothered him about Dean. He looked away, moving his hands across his face, wiping the perspiration from his eyes. He then bolted down the stairs after one last quick glance through the telescope, and ran down to the Broad Street side of the tower and looked down towards the Governor's house. He saw Dean running in. He was determined to speak with him before he left, or was captured. He went after him, running as fast as he could. He ran to the house and found Dean straightaway, rushing round grabbing things. It was clear he was in a state, stuffing his things in a small bag. Edward tried to get an answer from him.

'Who are these people, Dean?' He stood over him and waited for a reply.

Dean answered quickly and incoherently as he put some boots on. 'Trouble for me, salvation for you.'

'That doesn't answer my question, does it? What kind of trouble?'

'Look, Edward, I'm on the run. Have been for years. I will

be executed if I get caught, so as much I'd like to stay and chat, I have to go and find a way out.' Tears began to flow from his eyes. Clearly in distress, his shaking almost uncontrollable. He paused for the second time to control it. Edward knelt down in front of him. 'I'm fed up with this,' Dean said, wiping the tears away. 'Tell Sheila something good. Don't tell her the truth, will you?'

'What shall I tell her?' he asked.

'Tell her I'm helping the authorities find a fugitive. As Governor,' Dean added, as an afterthought.

'Okay. I'll tell her whatever you want.'

Dean walked across the room, as Edward stood and watched him. He threw on the large coat he'd arrived in. They went down the stairs and into the street and Edward shadowed him, like a loyal dog worried his owner would leave him alone. Eventually he came to a halt and watched as he ran quickly down Broad Street out of town. He was now left to deal with these invaders. Edward ran back through the alley next to the tower, and out towards the plains, spotting a soldier on the way. He ducked inside against the alley wall, and watched secretly as an officer spotted Dean. As Edward hid, he listened to the soldier's radio. The soldier knelt down, to broadcast Dean's position. Surely Dean was caught? Edward crept forward almost on his hands and knees, and reached inside his jacket for the pencil he knew was there. The soldier was kneeling down looking through a pair of binoculars. Edward carefully unscrewed the antenna from the soldier's radio strapped on his back and lodged his last pencil there instead, jamming it into the socket. He thought about breaking it off, but wasn't confident he could do it without getting caught. The soldier unsuccessfully radioed in, his earphones belting out a litany of tinny noises, his voice repeating the message several times as Edward crept back. Once inside the alley he walked quickly, then broke into a run. He headed back towards the plain, where the entire army had landed. Edward watched, mesmerised by the amount of vehicles rolling across the plain, dust everywhere, craft hovering above; some landing, some flying around. An army jeep stopped in front of him as the others roared past. Out of it came six more men, dressed in uniform, and armed with a side arm, a large automatic weapon and a utility belt full of equipment. The lead officer spoke up.

'You, sir! Do you understand me?'

'Yes,' Edward replied.

'Good,' he said, 'Now listen. We're looking for a fugitive named Michael Dean'. He pulled out a photograph.

As Edward took it from him, his hand shook. Thoughts raced through his mind about how much information this was giving away to the officer. Was he just scared or guilty?

'I want you to take this photo to your Governor and then I will come and speak to him later this afternoon. Do you understand?'

'I am the Governor,' Edward explained in a small voice. He tried to remember his conversation with Dean – 'trouble for me, salvation for you' – running it through his head to steady his nerves. There was a very uncomfortable silence, as the officer stared at him as if to read his body language.

'Right, come with me.' His voice made Edward jump. He motioned two of his men and they hauled him into the jeep. Edward didn't struggle. They drove, on Edward's instruction, to the hall. When he got out of the jeep, he looked behind him and saw at least a hundred men, all dressed in black, climbing out of jeeps with aircraft above. He was frightened for his life and the lives of his community. They weren't friendly. They were clearly aggressive. As more men appeared at the entrance of the hall, people looked startled as dozens of soldiers poured in and began instructing people to move to the back wall; guns raised against them, shouting instructions at the top their voices. The people here would never have resisted. Edward stood next to the soldiers looking dour, his head slightly bowed. He looked across the hall, as the hall began filling up with equipment. The soldiers pushed past Edward from their vehicles, carrying boxes, furniture and weapons. As the men came in, they took people to be questioned and processed, a number of soldiers holding clipboards, with armed guards next to them. Edward was ignored for a moment, as the Captain he'd spoken to seemed to be more interested in asking where the Governor was than taking him at his word. The

Captain either hadn't heard what he'd said, or didn't believe him. It was probably for the best. He slipped away, while he had the chance, back to the tower to salvage his things.

As he arrived soldiers were pouring in and out of the tower as well, already moving in equipment and gadgets, men crawling everywhere, and taking everything they needed quickly and efficiently. Edward slipped in past them and ran up to get his telescope. As he reached the third floor a soldier met him and placed his hand against his chest. Edward looked down at the hand and up at the face, partly covered by a helmet and visor. What was he going to do? He told him to turn round and head back to the hall. He went back downstairs as the soldier motioned to two men and he was frogmarched back into the hall, where the Captain spotted him. He was led over to see a more senior officer, while everyone was questioned in rows, like a census. The thin drawn faces of the people stared up at him, white and unhappy. Edward looked at them as they all looked backed at him. They stood completely silent, unsure what to do for the best, except do as they were asked. Names were taken and then they were moved along the line to have photos taken and biometric information was removed and added to their databases. The people were silent and passive. It was hard to gauge what they were thinking. Did they assume that they were central government come to liberate them from isolation? Edward stood and waited, as the soldier's hand tightly clutched his coat. He had half a mind to wriggle free and make a dash for it, but his priority was here, to go through what his friends and family were going through. To be there for them.

A general had already taken centre stage, his ego filling the hall. He had a desk, monitors and communications set up with wires sprawled across the floor, as men came and went, bringing things and going off on errands. The community's own desk and stand had been thrown to one side. Edward was frogmarched up to the General and was questioned. The General was short and stout, with a beard, with dark, piercing eyes. A man with intelligence and patience, but decisive.

'You know this man?' He spoke sharply, holding up a photo

of Dean, as if it was a closed question, with only one possible answer.

'Yes, that's Dean,' Edward replied.

'Michael Dean?'

'We only knew him as Dean.'

'Do you know this man is a vicious mercenary and fugitive?'

'No I did not,' Edward told him.

'You and your people have been assisting a fugitive. You'll be held here, until we find him. Do you know where he's gone?' the General asked.

'Not a clue,' Edward replied.

The General stood up. 'That's all for now. Please remain in the hall.'

'Who are you, if you don't mind me asking?'

'I am General Pickerton, from the Federation of Police Authorities.'

'You're from central government?' Edward asked.

'Central what?'

'British central government.'

'Sorry, there is no government here. Hasn't been for a long time,' the General explained.

'I don't understand. You are from...where? What country?' Edward was now seriously confused. What had been going on out there? Did the British government no longer exist?

The General ignored him, waving him off the stage and back down with the others as if irritated by him. Edward was stumped, baffled by this sudden revelation. Central government was dead, and these men? Had technology gone forward so quickly that the craft they use seemed alien, the equipment Dean had used on the plain not of this earth? It all seemed other-worldly, unusual for a country in such dramatic decline. He needed to find some answers. The confusion raged around him as the frantic activity continued at a pace Edward could barely comprehend. He needed to find Dean. But first he went to find Madeline.

He found her pacing up and down between the kitchen and hall. 'Edward. Who are these people?' She said this before Edward had reached her.

He looked into her frightened eyes, filled with tears that had not yet fallen. 'They say they're from some kind of federation.'

'What federation? Where is our government?' She shook, tears flowing freely from her face, Simon clinging to her legs.

'I know you must have a lot of questions, but I just don't know any answers.' Edward lifted his voice above the din, as others started to walk over to him, as soldiers moved men back into line. Women shouted and cried, their long hair coming loose, becoming strewn across swollen tearful faces. It was as distressing as an enemy invasion. These military men couldn't possibly be here to help. They were here to destroy Dean and anyone who knew him.

'They're all saying we're in trouble for helping Dean. That can't be right, can it?' Madeline protested.

'I don't think we've got much of a choice.'

'But he's a good man. What could he have done?'

Madie was as confused as he was. But he did not profess to have any answers for her. The situation had quickly become unbearable. They hugged briefly. Simon hugged them both, bringing a smile.

'Dad, what have we done?' Simon asked.

Edward had no answers for him either. He was already resigned to the fact that Dean was gone and these men were here in his place. He had brought them here. That was the bottom line.

A soldier passed, briefly looking at him, perhaps under orders to watch him. The three of them were huddled together, with a soldier or two hovering round them, their presence keeping the others away. How badly would they be treated as the first family? It was hard to see what Dean had been saying.

Simon needed reassuring. So far he was a little bewildered, but tears would come eventually. 'It's all right, Simon.' Edward patted him awkwardly. 'They're just a bit annoyed with us. We're not in trouble.' Edward picked him up and hugged him as he played with Edward's face and hair.

'This is our home!' They all jumped to the sound of the hall suddenly filled with a woman's voice. They looked for her and Edward recognised Lileth. He then decided to take Madeline and Simon upstairs to their room and the soldiers followed.

He closed the door slowly as the soldier stood right outside his door. The door clicked shut and he turned to see Madeline getting on with things, tidying and sorting. It was just like her to make herself busy. Edward would probably sit and brood.

They were allowed to stay in the apartment that night, but Edward barely slept at all, and by the early hours he was still pacing up and down, waiting for first light. The crying and arguing had kept him awake, as he waited to be questioned. A silence occurred between them, a gap, which remained undefined, Edward not knowing if she was annoyed with him or not. Not wanting to ask, unsure about her answer. She might lie or she might tell the truth. Both were equally frightening to him. They waited as if waiting to see a doctor, with little to say. He wanted to comfort her, reassure her, but he could not. He could offer no guarantees at all. But by 3.30 in the morning, it had finally gone quiet. Madeline was asleep, but he woke her to tell her he was going to find Dean. She agreed, understanding him immediately. She wanted to know more and they both knew the others would want to.

The night was lit up by search lights and flood lamps lighting up whole streets while tanks rolled along, with the occasional loud bang, shaking the ground, usually followed by a deep rumbling sound which Edward could only presume would be collapsing buildings. He went out to one of the balconies and looked out over the town. He was shocked by the devastation being caused in the search for Dean. It was incredible. The town was being raised to the ground. Buildings raged with fire, engulfing them sending them into oblivion. Buildings that had been in use when he was a child. One by one people came and joined him on balcony. Below him people came outside, braced by the soldiers holding them back. Madie came out to him as well clutching Simon in her arms, not wanting to leave him behind. Edward went down to the street.

'Let me through!' he demanded. 'I want to speak to your commanding officer immediately! I am the Governor of this town. I want to know why you're currently destroying it!' he yelled. They let him through. He could see General Pickerton with his back to him, his hands pointing at sections of the town, a bank of computer monitors, in front of him with a flimsy water proof canvas over them. He saw an officer whisper something in his ear as Edward approached him and turned around to face him.

'Governor Kingston. Come and join us,' he turned back and as he did he beckoned him forward with a friendly wave of his hand, obviously keen to share the exploits of a violent army hell bent on raising Goscote to the ground.

'You see, the ground troops go in, do a preliminary search, the tanks move in to destroy the building, then move on. We pinned down this whole town by satellite days ago. Any creature that moves will be picked up by our heat sensitive cameras, and any movement at all reported to our operations centre, then passed on to us. Not even a rat could escape.'

'General, do you really need Dean so much you have to raise this small town to the ground?' Edward was not interested in military methods, camera's and satellites.

'I think if you realised who you were protecting you wouldn't be so concerned. This town is dead, its buildings are dangerously close to collapse. Surely this helps you?'

'By destroying our town?'

'Don't you realise this whole country is a waste land of fugitives running from the Federation, dying communities no bigger than yours, and roaming groups of bandits and vagabonds. The Federation will bring order and civilisation back to Britain. You'll have a working government within months. Transportation, trade and whole towns will come back to life.'

'What did Dean do anyway?' Edward looked over at him waiting for his reply, wondering if the Federation, whoever they were had lost their minds.

'I can't tell you that,' the general replied.

'Of course you can't. Anyway, whatever the reason is, it still doesn't explain why you've brought all this hardware. I mean you've virtually invaded, all for one man.' The two men stood in silence for a while, as the troops, tanks and helicopters searched the town. 'Well you let me know if you find him. I'd like to ask him a few things myself.' The General turned sharply to Edward, as if he'd hit a raw nerve.

'Be under no illusions Mr Kingston. You and your friends are in a lot of trouble. There are laws in this town, just as there are any where else the Federation has a presence. And you will be put on trial for harbouring a terrorist.' Edward didn't answer. He just looked away and stared into the eyes of his new enemy before he returned to Madeline and the others.

'Well?' Mrs Edmunds said, in her usual impatient way, her arms tightly crossed across her chest. Madie glared at her when she said that. Her arms then crossed, waiting to retaliate should she begin to blame poor Edward, who was trying his best.

'He is "searching" for Dean,' Edward said, signing speech marks with his hands.

'Why though?' one of the girls said. 'What has he done?'

'I asked, but the general wouldn't tell me.'

'Oh great!' Madeline exclaimed. 'That's all we need.' The group broke up and returned to their rooms, but no one expected to get any sleep that night.

Edward looked at his watch unable to focus, as the banging started at the door. 'Soldiers, I expect,' Edward said to Madeline across the small space in between them, in their bed. She smiled, got out of bed, throwing on her dressing gown, and walking through to wake Simon. Edward waited to open the door, watching to see when Madeline was ready to be seen, as she dressed. She nodded, and he opened the door. The soldiers ordered his attendance.

'You are required to see the General, sir. Can you come with me?' They reached in and grabbed him.

'I'm not dressed. What are you going to do? March me down to the General in my nightclothes?' He argued, as he was grabbed by the arms on each side and walked down the corridor. 'Hang on!' He struggled, as another soldier followed them. A senior officer watching from further down the corridor intervened, ordering him to allow Edward to dress.

'As soon as you're ready, Edward.' The officer looked at him with an intimidating stare, as if to threaten both him and the subordinate soldiers. Edward walked back in, softly closing the door behind him. He pressed his back against the door, his heart racing. He looked up at Madeline and looked coldly at her, trying to hide his fear. She tightened her dressing gown, her arms folding tightly, hunching her shoulders from the humiliation and the cold. Edward walked into the second room and dressed quickly, covering his embarrassment with frantic activity.

'You don't have to go now, Edward. Just wait. Take your time. Show them you won't be intimidated,' she ordered.

'I am intimidated.' He looked up at her, fear showing in his face now, trying not to tremble. He wanted her to understand, unable to describe his isolation. 'I wish my father and brother were here. I'm the Governor again. I'm twenty-one. I'm too young to take all this.'

'Mr Workman will be there.' Madeline tried to offer some hope.

'Mr Workman,' Edward replied, sarcastically. 'Let's hope Joe's there as well then.' She scowled at him. Edward felt on his own even though Madeline saw Mr Workman and Joe as being on hand. But the reality was very different. Mr Workman had stayed quiet, and clearly wasn't up to the job of dealing with the soldiers and since the soldiers arrived Joe had barely spoken to him. It was clear there was some resentment over who invited Dean in. It was Edward and although no one had said anything directly – perhaps not having had a chance – Edward felt sure that this was what they were thinking. He didn't want to share this suspicion with Madie, for fear it would spark off a debate he didn't want to take part in. There was a mood of blame sweeping the people, and even if it wasn't there, Edward felt sure he could see it in their faces. He was not going to invite accusations by starting to talk about it with Madie or anyone else.

Edward braced himself and opened the door to the soldier, as he glared at Madeline standing inside the tiny apartment. The minute Edward stepped out he was grabbed by each arm, and marched downstairs. As he turned into the hall, he could see soldiers talking to residents over desks and tables, soldiers walking around talking into phones, tapping into computers and printers whirring, as they spewed out paper. They walked past all of this, out onto the street, past three buildings between the hall and the Governor's house, and in through the door and up the stairs. Edward glanced in as they passed Dean's old apartment, trying to see if he was there. He could hear aircraft passing overhead. Roaring engines echoed in the background, sometimes making the building shake. He hoped he would see him there, being questioned, the General could be told the truth and they would be freed. But instead he saw two soldiers and some civilians searching through Dean's things, but no Dean.

As they arrived at the second-floor apartment, he noticed immediately how the place had been stripped of all its furniture, fixtures and fittings. The place had been whitewashed, and had a woman in uniform sitting at a desk. He could hear a man talking from the other room, through the huge double doors, who he assumed would be the General. Edward was forced into the waiting-room chairs by the soldier's hand and asked to wait.

Then he was called in.

'Edward. Sit down.'

Edward sat, and looked silently at the General. The big man went straight into it, firing statements at him: 'You, and your people, will be charged with assisting a fugitive. I think you already know that.' Edward nodded, trying not to look or feel weakened by this intimidating man. 'This means you will face a court, and will be dealt with under Federation law.'

'I don't know what the Federation laws are,' Edward told the General. His concentration was going, his heart thumping, feeling the rush of adrenalin through his veins, his stomach churning.

The General marched on through the instructions, as generals do, ignoring the temptation to waffle, unchallenged by the small fearful man in front of him.

'You'll be assumed as Governor of Goscote, which means you will have to defend yourself and your town from the charges. The penalty could be as severe as death.' Edward looked unmoved by this, which was noted by the General, with a brief pause and a stare in the junior officer's direction. Edward was getting the better of his nerves. 'At best you could go to prison for an undetermined length of time, which will no doubt be a facility, built somewhere locally. I believe there is a prison being built as we speak. That is all.' He looked up and nodded at the soldier, as Edward was suddenly wrenched up from the chair, unaware that the end of the meeting was anywhere in sight. 'Oh, and all of you will be confined only to the Town Hall, the Governor's residence, which will be made available to you, and the Town Hall garden and allotment. You will be supplied with food, medicine, power and basic supplies.' As he talked, Edward wondered if this man was ever going to see the injustice unfolding here.

As Edward was pulled from the office he asked, 'Could I collect some things from the tower block?' trying his luck.

'Which things are these?' The General asked.

'A telescope and a couple of personal things I keep up on the seventh floor.'

The General looked at his officer. 'Can we locate these things, Sergeant?' he asked, looking up at the soldier. The General was human after all. Just the smallest of signs. Perhaps he was just in a good mood, or was a keen astronomer.

'I'm sure we can, sir.'

The General smiled at Edward, before he was accompanied back to the hall. Edward didn't want to jump to a conclusion about this man. It occurred to him that he should culture a friendship with him. Even if it didn't have a major payoff, there would be advantages. It would be harder to punish him, and would help if Edward found himself defending the actions of one of the members of the town. All this he considered, feeling pleased with himself for having thought of it.

Edward arrived back sooner than expected and was greeted by a hug, from Madeline. 'What happened in there, Edward?' she asked.

'We're all being put on trial for assisting a fugitive and the penalty will be death or prison.'

'Oh, Lord!' Madeline covered her face with her hands. 'He assisted us! I don't understand. What else was said?' she dared to ask.

Edward sat on the bed, with his chin resting on his hands. 'I've been appointed as Governor; officially... .' He looked up at Madeline in disgust, sighed and said, 'Which means it's my responsibility to provide a defence for everyone.' He thought for a second. Had he really connected with General Pickerton, because it was vital that he did? It would occupy his thoughts until he had a chance to speak with him again. He felt sure it was his best chance to overcome these difficulties.

'Oh, it gets worse!' Madeline exclaimed after pausing for a second, as if unable to think through what she'd just been told, needing time to relay it in her head. 'What about poor Sheila?' Madie asked.

'Oh no! I forgot about Sheila!' He jumped up, 'I'll have to find her straightaway. Look, Madeline, you have to tell everyone that they are not to say she's Dean's wife. Make sure you tell everyone, I'm relying on you.'

'What if the General already knows?' she asked.

'I'll go and find her now.' Edward rushed out as Madeline grabbed Simon and walked out after Edward, bumping into Sarah, May and Janice at the bottom of the stairs, while Edward used the banister to sling himself round to head off to the back of the hall.

Edward quickly found Sheila, in the furthest shed, the one that Dean built. As he arrived he could hear her sobbing. He waited for a second or two and then knocked gently. The sobbing stopped, as if she was in there frozen to the spot with fear, not knowing who it was. There was a clunk and then the door swung out and there she was sitting alone, her face covered in dark stripes from her tears. Edward crept in and crouched down in front of her, and reached out an arm to comfort her. They hugged.

'Don't tell them, Edward, but I'm pregnant.'

'Oh, no.' Edward knew this was bad news. Sheila could be in serious jeopardy. How would the Federation treat her, if they were to find out?

'We need to make sure that the Federation doesn't know who you are, Sheila. Being pregnant isn't good, but we'll think of something, okay? Look, you weren't married to Dean. That way we'll keep you well away from the trials.'

'Trials?' Sheila asked. Edward was hoping for a chance that they hadn't realised the two of them were married. No connection could have been made, unless someone had said something. 'What do you mean, I wasn't married? I was married. It will all come out,' she said, resigned to the worst.

'Didn't the soldiers tell you about the trial?'

She shook her head. 'What have we done to deserve this?' She wiped her eyes and straightened up. She was sitting on a metal drum, her knees knocking with fear and emotion, her hands shaking, with a blanket and thin mattress at the back of the shed.

'You need to come back in,' Edward explained.

'No,' she said. 'Where did I get this baby from, if I'm not married?'

'That's a good point.' Edward thought for a while. Sheila would be in huge trouble if he didn't come up with an answer. He sat crouched down on the cold floor, looking at her, wondering how she'd managed to stay in there, with the freezing temperatures. She may well lose the baby if she doesn't come inside.

'We're a religious community, Edward. How are we going to explain?' she whined.

Edward made use of the adrenalin positively this time, as ideas began to pop into his head. He was beginning the think on his feet. 'Take off your ring and hide it. We'll think of something. You'll have to keep a low profile, do you under-stand? Don't talk to me, Joe, May, Madeline or anyone close to Dean. Keep away, as if you barely know us. You're friends with Debbie's girls, aren't you?'

'Yes,' she replied. Debbie was a middle-aged woman who had three girls. The girls had four kids between them and when Debbie died, the town had a huge funeral. Hers was the last large family and was well liked by everyone.

'You stay with Debbie's girls, and you tell them what I told you. Stay away from all of us who were Dean's friends and you'll be fine.'

'What about the baby?' she asked.

Edward didn't know what to say to her. He thought for a second. 'These soldiers won't know the dynamics of the town – who's married to whom. Your marriage to Dean was never recorded, remember?' She nodded. 'If you sort out between you and Debbie's girls how you're going to cover things, then I won't know, will I? I won't know, so that will help our story, about the connection with each other. We are just about big enough in population to get away with it I reckon.' She smiled through her tears, and nodded. 'And the baby? I'd find a pretend husband. I reckon it would be easier to admit to having an affair with one of Debbie's girls' husbands, than to say it's Dean's child and you're his wife. Anyway you might be clear of this place before they know you're even pregnant.' She nodded again. This was the best he could do for now. Keep her away from the main group of Dean's friends and hope the General and his men didn't realise. Edward got up and hugged her. He turned to leave too quickly. She wanted to talk.

'Dean built this shed.'

He turned back. 'I know,' he said, smiling. 'I guessed you might be here. How long have you been hiding?'

'Only this morning.'

'What about before that?'

'I just kept moving around, looking for Dean. I felt so helpless. Pathetic, isn't it? I just want to die really. Why did he do this to us, Edward? We didn't deserve it.'

How was he going to defend him? 'I know. He needed a place to hide and he tried to pay us back with kindness, showing us a thing or two.'

'What happened to him then?' she asked.

Edward considered telling a lie. 'He got away,' he blurted out. 'I don't suppose we'll see him again. You'll have to get used to it, Sheila.' Better be straight with her.

'I know.' She wiped her tears away.

Edward moved to the door to poke his head out to see if it was clear. He said goodbye, asking her to wait for a while. An hour at least, making sure she moved the bedding and any indication she'd been there. He left her, taking some of her things to dump, in case she was caught. He walked down through the allotments, back round the side of the building, to make sure none of the soldiers had seen him. He then came out onto Broad Street and stopped outside the Governor's house. He looked up and stood still for a second, soldiers pushing past him, going about their business.

'Ah, Governor!' The Sergeant spotted him, making him jump. 'Your office is being prepared upstairs.'

'Which floor?' Edward asked.

'Top!' The Sergeant replied, a smile on his face, as if he'd just given Edward some good news. Governor Westbrook's old digs. He didn't want to stay there, but he'd have to. They climbed the stairs.

'Follow me, I'll show you round.' As if he didn't know. They climbed the stairs, trying to avoid small talk. How could they be friendly, when they were about to condemn him?

They arrived at the top floor, and the same process had happened here as with the General's office. Whitewashed, with basic phone and desk, chairs for waiting and a computer. 'There will be one of the admin staff along soon to talk you through things,' he was told.

Edward walked around nervously, sitting at the desk as the Sergeant left. Edward stood up and went to the window. He looked across the old town, as a hive of activity took place below. The birds still circling around aimlessly like that last day he'd spent with the Governor. The rubble was being torn down, dust rising up into the sky, plant vehicles moving in every direction. As Edward looked closer, he could see a wall was being constructed around the house, the allotment and the hall. Horrified, he moved quickly across to the other side of the office to look down over the garden, and there the same scene. He couldn't believe it. A ghetto. Goscote, his home for his whole life, and his father's life, was being turned into a ghetto. It was a major crisis. He had no resources to fight these men. He had no clue how to fight. He was alone and desperate, knowing that Madeline would pull out all the stops to care for him. But there was no fighting spirit here. It was a simple place. He looked across the other side of the building leaning on the window sill, watching a few distant buildings being torn down, and noting what others were left standing; trying to work out what was there when he was growing up. He couldn't figure out what they were. Bulldozers and plant could be seen. It took a few seconds to locate the wall among the other buildings, his eyes darting across the landscape, constructing in his mind's eye the work being done. His home was being converted into a prison. This was going to get a lot tougher. The admin clerk turned up jolting him from his daze. He was shown how to use the telephone and computer system, his mind turning to the job at hand. He could not process all of what was happening and for now this would do to distract him.

By late afternoon he returned to Madeline and they sat down together and discussed the day's business like a married couple. It was the first time that either of them could remember being like that with each other. Sharing responsibilities, discussing problems and airing grievances. Simon sat like a little angel, perched on the end of the chair, his legs dangling from the edges, his little round shoes barely reaching the floor. He just sat silently and listened. Madeline and Edward both stopped and looked at him. Then he noticed they were smiling at him, and smiled back. They looked at each other. They soon stopped smiling when the gravity of what was happening returned to their minds. They felt condemned. The wall had been constructed before the trial, a sure sign of a verdict already decided. Then they continued talking, moving on to Sheila. Both agreed not to discuss her anymore, even privately, in case they were being monitored by the General. With sadness, they wished her well, lighting a candle to her, the baby and Dean, and then they slept.

CHAPTER EIGHT

As the days passed, the paperwork flowed endlessly. Edward tried to keep up with the high volume of information, but feared mistakes and omissions would be made, affecting real lives. Madeline and Simon moved into the Governor's house and she took the role of secretary and counsel. The General kept in touch and they often met to discuss individual cases. But the General was not much of a negotiator. Everything was black and white to him and Edward soon realised he would have to toughen up quickly, to take him on. One morning the General came to get him, dragging him out of bed at five a.m. Disgruntled by the interruption Edward was sure he had no means of escape, as the General's guards were with him, and in no mood to be shooed away. But Edward was surprised to hear the General's cheerful announcement once he'd got up.

'I want to take you to the officers' canteen this morning as we have a few things to discuss. I'm sure you can manage a Federation breakfast.' He spun round on his foot, like a thousand Saturday morning square-bashing sessions. The rule of the march, determining his every step. Edward struggled to keep up with the older man as he marched off towards the plains and dipped his head into a giant tent. He walked through with every passing soldier obediently saluting. They arrived in the tent, and the officers eating breakfast stood up and saluted until they were told to carry on eating. They sat down noisily as several of them stared rudely at Edward, having never been this close to him. He was aware for the first time of his status here. The General went straight into an anecdote about his wife, as Edward sat and listened wondering what the hell this was all about. Just as he thought that, the General skilfully turned his attention to Edward:

'I suppose you're wondering what the hell this is all about?'

'Yes,' Edward replied. 'I was just thinking that very thing. That's not to say your anecdote about your wife wasn't fascinating.'

The other soldiers went white and looked horrified as the words left Edward's mouth. As his confidence grew, Edward began to try to push his luck, and test the boundaries, which the General let him do. The fact was he was going easy on him.

The General asked his men to leave him after that and turned to Edward. 'If you were one of my soldiers you'd be in trouble for saying that. But you're not one of my soldiers, and I realise you are probably keen to find out what I've brought you here for. The truth is I like telling those stories and enjoy watching people pretend to enjoy them. I know the sycophants from the truth tellers then. And you, my young friend, are a truth teller,' and he pointed. 'The kind of people I want around me. I've seen better soldiers than me surround themselves with yes men. They all end up making mistakes.'

'I don't know, General, whether you're our friend or our enemy. The fact is we were looking at the final generation in Goscote. We were a decade or two away from extinction. Perhaps you could tell me if you're a friend or an enemy?'

'I'm a soldier doing my job.'

'If you're a soldier doing your job, you should be able to tell the difference between a friend and an enemy.'

'That's if you discount politics, Edward.'

'Right.'

The two men stared at each other for a while, before Edward was interrupted by one of the waiters pouring tea into his empty cup, and took the opportunity to look away. It was an uneasy standoff. By the end of the second week, sixty-two members of Goscote were to face charges, some lesser than others. The two men had spent time together, enough to know that given different circumstances they might have made good colleagues; maybe even friends. But here they were sorting people into two groups, which would determine whether they lived or died. And by his hand, the General would probably oversee the executions of those added to the 'kill list', as it became known, Edward's name included together with poor Madeline's. The rest Edward successfully squared away onto the release schedule. Sheila's name was kept out of it and Edward never mentioned her. She came up on the paperwork once or twice, but no one said a word. She was a minor member of the community, far removed from the hub of Dean's work and relationships. Whenever he saw her name, he never read the details. He passed it on, signed or stamped whatever he had to do, to keep her name moving down the columns to the release schedule, ready for the trials at the beginning of the following month. The date was set for the end of January.

The regular meetings meant that as their working relationship grew Edward spent more time within the inner circle of officers, in the officers' mess. It was a great arena for learning leadership skills, listening more carefully than the General ever realised, to the stories about insubordinate soldiers and the ongoing battle to survive. News from HQ was particularly fascinating, which meant often changing the subject when they suddenly realised Edward was listening. Even though these men and women did an excellent job in keeping themselves well financed and well fed, survival was everyone's concern. It wasn't just about small cut-off communities like Goscote. The problems they faced were the same, in big communities and small. Earth was being slowly suffocated by the cloud. It was everyone's problem.

At each session he attended he learned a little more about the General's life back home. He had two sons who resented him and a long-suffering wife, whom he didn't like. Every time she rang him he would grimace. The army was his life.

'What is the problem, General? Why don't you like your wife?' Edward asked one evening over a drink in the officers' mess, the mumbling sounds of the men in the background, the occasional sound of a helicopter flying overhead.

'I just think she would be better off without me. I don't hate her. In the old days when I went away it would take weeks to get used to being without her. Over the years we've grown apart for obvious reasons. Now I see this as my home, not home.'

'I love my wife. I hope I never get to that stage, but I know how you feel. I used to go up to the tower to get away from everyone, before you closed it down.'

'It's not a safe structure anymore.'

'That's all right. I don't care. It's a terrible piece of architecture anyway.'

The General laughed.

That night Edward returned late. Madeline hated him spending too much time with the General. She didn't understand. But bearing in mind what had been said earlier, he said he would stop drinking with him.

'He is the enemy.' She pointed at him as if he was standing next to them.

'I needed to get into a friendly relationship with him, to…'

'I know, you keep saying. We've got less than a month to get out of this, Edward. This is our last few days together before our family could be torn to pieces by your friend the General.'

Edward silently listened, his brow furrowed, the tension in his face showing. Then she suddenly stopped.

'You've finished?' he said.

'Yeah.' Her head bowed in shame for a second and then she stormed off into the bedroom and slammed the door. He thought back to the General and his wife. He had to stop attaching himself to these patriarchs. He was twenty-two. He'd been alone for a long time already; without a father, a priest, a leader to look to for advice. He'd looked to weak ineffective men, like a child looking for a father to show him how to be a man. Madeline had given him more valuable advice than the old Governor, or Mr Workman who had always resented him.

That night he slept on the couch.

On the morning of 12th January 2134, Edward woke up and saw Madeline shuffling around in her dressing gown, looking for something to do. They had long since made up for their arguments. Edward explained to the General that it was time they slipped into traditional roles and stopped mixing like colleagues. He felt he had to point out that they were on opposite sides and it wasn't going unnoticed by others in the Federation and in Goscote itself.

'Get up!' she said. 'I know you're awake.'

He turned over. 'Right oh,' he said. He got up and put on his dressing gown, Edward automatically doing as he was instructed, a smile on his face. Madeline was a good-natured woman, quiet most of the time. Intelligent all of the time. He loved her. He did what she wanted. She'd never asked him why he used to go missing sometimes and now it puzzled him. He suspected she knew all along; maybe even going up the tower to see for herself what was going on. He just didn't know for sure. Not many women would have coped with it. Perhaps she was glad of having the space? That morning he looked at her and realised for the first time she must have been up there to see what he was up to. Perhaps she was too embarrassed to mention it? It might have been uncomfortable for her to accept that her husband wanted to spend time on his own; hoping it would pass. And it had. Edward no longer feared feeling claustrophobic with her. It was the change in circumstances, he was sure of that. Now he loved being with her more than ever.

By 9.30 he was ready for the day ahead, glancing out the window at the allotment, now falling into disarray given the food supplies coming from the Federation. The bulldozed buildings, the ones left behind, the piles of rubble, spread randomly across the landscape, seemed so pathetically apocalyptic. Like a failed attempt at the end of the world; a half-hearted destroyer of life, which had hardly bothered to finish the job it had started. He sat at his breakfast table with a hot drink waiting for Madie to serve up some food. Periodically, well a great deal of the time, he wondered what the General knew about Dean. 'Do you think he killed someone important to the Federation?' he asked Madie.

'What?' she said.

'Dean. Do you think he killed someone famous or something?' Madie came into the room with some food for both of them. She'd already fed Simon.

'Yeah. He must have done something terrible,' Madie said.

'Do you think that the General would have a file on him in his office?' Edward asked.

'I guess so. Why?'

'I noticed that they take the guards downstairs at night, nowhere near the apartment. I could break in.'

'Yeah, great idea Ed. They'd know it was you straight away. You'd get into trouble.'

'I'm not sure I would get into that much trouble. I could just do it then admit it and say, 'so what?' he said with a look of defiance, as if practicing. 'We have a right to know.'

'We do have a right to know. I agree.'

'What do you think then? Shall I?' he asked. Madie stopped eating, holding a piece of toast in her hand. Although it wasn't proper toast. Just an unleavened bread warmed up a little, with some fat on it.

'Yeah. Do it. I might come with you,' she added with a smile.

'No. That wouldn't be a good idea. Who'd look after Simon if we both got taken away?'

'True,' she said. And that was settled. Later that night when the office was locked up and empty he would break in and see what was what.

He left the apartment and headed downstairs to his office. He had to pass the General's office to get to it. As he passed the open door of the General's office, he heard him bellow his name. 'Edward!' he shouted, in a deep booming voice, he probably used that same voice to bellow at insubordinate soldiers, he thought. Edward cringed and turned round and headed into the apartment.

'You bellowed,' he said, defiantly.

'I did. The trial starts soon Edward. When it does I will be leaving and a civilian will take my place. A chap called Young. You'll be reporting to him.'

'Reporting? I'm not one of your soldiers,' Edward replied. The General looked him up and down in disgust.

'Okay. Well I'm just telling you.'

'Fine,' Edward said and left.

That night at nine he left the apartment with a crowbar and climbed down the stairs to the General's office. As predicted the apartment wasn't guarded. He gave it a push with his hands just to see how much give there was. He looked closely at the lock, then inserted the sharp edge of the crow bar into the gap between the lock and the door frame. The frame cracked and moaned, as he lifted if from its placement. He then increased the effort and the door sprung open and hit the back of the wall. He walked in and closed the door to. He walked straight into the General's office, to the filing cabinet which was also locked. He lifted a small screw driver from his pocket and jimmied it open, taking a few minutes to get the better of it. The drawer sprung open like the door did, when it finally succumbed to Edward's screw driver. He fingered through the files and found what he was looking for. He picked it up out of the cabinet and left the apartment and hurried up the stairs to his where Madeline waited for him, perched nervously on the edge of one of the dining table chairs. As he entered she stood up and Edward opened the file and spread it out on the table. They both poured over it, hunched over the table. 'We'll have to get some of the others to come over and look at this,' Edward suggested.

'Yeah. But I wonder whether it helps us to know what he did,' Madie said.

'What do you mean?'

'Well, we're being accused of harbouring a terrorist right?'

'Yeah.'

'If we know nothing about him, then that supports our assertion that he never told us anything. If everyone knows what he did then that looks like we helped him doesn't it?'

'Yeah I suppose it does.' Edward and Madie silently looked at the papers in front of them. 'I guess I ought to take this back. Now we know what we wanted to know. Even those strange aircraft he had are in here.'

'Yeah, take it back and put it on his desk in the middle. Send him a message.' Madie suggested.

'Oh, I'm sure not about that.'

'Well, where else are you going to put it? Back in the filing cabinet?'

'Think about it Madie. If I put it back in the filing cabinet he won't know for sure which document we looked at.'

'True,' she concurred.

'That means we have deniability.'

'But weren't you going to admit it?' Edward looked down feeling a little confused as to the best course of action.

'No. I think I'll put it back in the file. That way I have the option of deniability.'

'Okay,' she said and smiled and put her hand on his shoulder for a second or two, before he stood up straight and left the apartment back to the office.

CHAPTER NINE

By 9.30 the following morning he was ready for the day ahead, glancing out the window at the allotment. There had been no recriminations from breaking into the General's office at all. Edward was a little surprised, but at the same time he suspected the General might be okay about it, given that he wasn't officially allowed to tell them what Dean had done.

Depressed by the scenes from his window he went downstairs past the General's office. The door was open a little. He wasn't all that surprised but he thought he'd have a little look anyway. He pushed the door gently. Inside was an empty apartment, stripped once more of its contents. Shocked, he walked in and through to the General's office; also empty. He looked around briefly before turning and going back upstairs.

'Madie the General's gone. The office has gone as well. He did say some guy called Young was taking his place.'

'What?' Madie said.

'He's cleared out his office. If he's moved on then I doubt we'll be in trouble for taking that file on Dean.'

'Cool. You thought you might get away with it. Well that's helpful isn't it? Perhaps this is ready for the trials?' she suggested. 'Go down to the hall. See what's happening there.'

He gathered his things together, shoving papers under his arm and headed for the hall. When he arrived, the hall had been arranged for the trials. He couldn't hide his dismay. There was an official standing there, dressed in a suit, barking orders at people, holding a pile of stapled papers. He kept referring to it as he spoke. Edward stood looking at him until the official noticed him. He stared at Edward, in an unfriendly uncompromising way. So Edward walked up to him.

'I'm Edward, the Governor. What's happening? Where's the General?'

'Governor Kingston. Nice to meet you,' he said sarcastically. He was slightly camp; a personality trait Edward had rarely come across. He was a young man. Slim, with black hair. Well educated and pale. 'I am Christopher Young. I have taken over. The General has left for a new assignment. There are several things I need to discuss with you. Come with me.'

They went out of the hall and into an office where the admin staff and the new civilian official running the trial had set up his office. They sat down looking at each other over the desk, Edward having a feeling he'd been here before. 'When the trial begins you will have to plead guilty or not guilty. If you plead not guilty you will have to face the death penalty, if found guilty by the court.'

'I'll have no choice?' Edward asked.

'You'll have no choice,' he repeated, methodically. He leant forward to labour the point, to underline his authority. 'You'll also be pleading for all of you, sixty-two in all.'

'Including children?' Edward said anxiously.

'Children will be taken into care.'

'What! You're kidding. They could stay with the other people being released, couldn't they?' A feeling of great anxiety welled up inside him, thinking immediately of poor Madie and how she'd cope if she lost Simon to the Federation.

'I doubt it,' Young explained coldly, a look of innate smugness crossing his face, as if he was always like this. He was enjoying it. Only a sadistic man would revel in these terrible measures.

Edward folded his arms, leaning in to engage his opponent in the conversation. 'And what if we plead guilty?'

'Death penalty, Edward, I've already said.'

'This is outrageous. What about the jury?' He was becoming more animated now.

'Three judges will sit.'

'From where?' Edward asked.

'From the Federation,' Young replied in that same methodical, disinterested tone.

Edward took in a deep breath. 'This is all very weighted in

your favour. Do you realise that the people of Goscote don't even know what Dean – that is, Michael – did to become a fugitive?'

'That's a matter for the court to decide.'

'Governor. This is a fact. No one knew who he was, until the Federation turned up.'

The Governor shrugged.

Edward got up and left in disgust.

'Goodbye, Governor Kingston,' Young said looking down at his notes as he spoke.

Edward didn't answer as he walked out. This was bad news. Very bad news. He quickly returned to the Governor's house, crossing the street quickly, glancing up at the wall that was getting higher. He took in a sigh. They clearly wanted to intimidate him with this wall. Make it seem as if the trial was predetermined. A fate already decided by someone far removed from the hall, from him and from the people here. Perhaps that's why they'd sent that awful man? All these thoughts raced through his mind, in the few short minutes it took to get back to the office, sit down and pick up the telephone. He would ring the General and check what Young had said. Find out if it was true.

General Pickerton and Edward had got on quite well up until now. He closed the office door so that Madie couldn't hear what he was doing. He rang the number of the operational command centre, asking where he could contact the General. He was put straight through.

'Edward! How are things?' the General asked.

'Do you know what's happening here?' he asked frantically.

'More or less,' he was unemotional about it.

'Do you know we face the death penalty, whichever way we plead?' he asked the General, making sure he knew how angry he was.

'This is for Chris Young to explain to you. I've been reassigned. But I will say one thing, which may help you.'

'What's that?' Edward replied, suspecting their friendship no longer counted for anything. He could no longer rely on his support.

'Young isn't there to oversee a fair trial.'

'No?' Edward's attitude changed.

'No. He's there to ensure that at least some of you do serious time for hiding Dean.'

Edward was stunned. He threw himself back in his chair. Silence followed while he took it all in. A second passed. 'You're telling me this is some kind of kangaroo court, with no chance of winning at all?'

'It's a stitch up, Edward. Look, I have to go. Good luck.' The phone went down.

'Good luck!' Edward shouted back. But he'd gone. 'Good luck!' Edward put the phone down. How was this useful to him? The trial was tomorrow. He thought he'd done everything he could to form a good defence, but now things were occurring to him that he hadn't thought of. Perhaps he should - they should boycott the trial?

He spent that entire night going through papers trying to read as much material as he could. Trying to commit things to memory, so he could fire off the facts if things got heated. But it all seemed so pointless. Madeline seemed to keep out of his way. He didn't know why, and had only one opportunity to ask, when he finally lay down next to her for some rest. But they just lay there silently, hardly speaking. She was wide-awake, as was he. But they had nothing to say. A couple of attempts at conversation were dashed by their obvious trivialness and so they silently let the state they were in hang there, because what could be said for facing the death penalty for no real reason? Surely it was obvious that they had no clue who Dean was. Surely there would be a consensus, that a fugitive would not offer the information, but it was not obvious to the Federation. These were all questions that should be answered tomorrow, and tomorrow was too far away for comfort, and too close to ignore. That night their thoughts were completely tied up in this. Of that there was no doubt. And as for Dean they never found him. Some how he'd managed to disappear. Whether he'd died in one of the hundred's of explosions, or whether he slipped away some how, no one really knew or understood, especially when they consider how much technology was used against him. Or the amount of ordnance used to make sure he was dead. It was all too much. Tomorrow he could be sentenced to death along with his wife and his closest friends. Friends who grew up with his father. Friends who cared for him when he had no one left.

The trial started the following day as the community gathered, Edward taking his place opposite the judges. They all looked at him and shuffled papers. The judges up on the stage, some officials including Christopher Young to his right, the people of Goscote behind him in chairs, Mr Workman and Joe with him at the front. The judges were dressed in strange judicial uniforms, red coats; no wigs, the middle seat missing its judge.

'All rise.' In came the primary judge as he took his seat. Edward nervously stood up. This was a nightmare.

As the court case proceeded without delay, Edward kept looking across at Chris Young, who grinned at him. The charges were read out and Edward pleaded not guilty to each, read out separately for each member of the community on their behalf. Edward defended everyone from outside Dean's immediate circle first, focusing on getting them out of harm's way as soon as possible. This was fairly straightforward with no major objections. He'd achieved this at least.

He explained that they were in little contact with Dean on a day-to-day basis, that the community had separate cliques, who rarely mingled, except on special occasions. He would have to prove it though. Edward had given this great thought. One by one he mentioned by name each member, and told the court with half a dozen examples that the inner circle would gather at night to spend time with him. He also explained that many of the people he had mentioned had separate growing areas for food, different sources of water, and differing methods of gathering resources, even down to the style in which clothes and furniture were made by them. It was a clear mark of difference he wanted to demonstrate. A way to show that the community, although living in one building, had led separate lives, in many ways. It was also a fact that three or more clans from the town had come together only three decades ago and not all the rivalries had fully disappeared. This he proved to the court, that by default they were not privy to any information about Dean's background, except that offered to them by Dean himself. The inner circle were the only ones privy to any information, which might indicate any involvement in covering up or hiding the fact that Dean was a mercenary and fugitive. By the end of the day, he had presented a sound case for most of the people on the General's list. Next, he would deal with the shorter list. The people who had spent time with him, enthralled by his stories.

That day came and went in a blur, as Edward rattled quickly and confidently through everything that needed to be said, answering every question and feeling satisfied that all witnesses had said exactly what they needed to say, with one or two exceptions. Edward had instructed many of them on how to handle things. The second day was also a blur. It came and went in the same fashion. In fact Edward was becoming concerned that it was too easy and as a consequence he was missing vital elements. He kept referring to his notes, his mind unable to locate the missing link that would make sense of it all. But he now prepared to defend those left. As he sat and thought through every word, he was convinced he'd done okay, but was worried he'd rushed it, going back over it in his mind, worried he'd only thought of himself. He hoped the others would be released. Hope was all that he had left. He wished it was over, but he must perform, he must slow down and understand every part of what was occurring. He was far too young for these responsibilities, but they were his alone.

His oratory continued apace. 'Many of the people on this list were enthralled and fascinated by his stories. But we never really knew who he was. Michael Dean invented stories, based on the way of life you defend,' he told the Federation judges, pointing at them. 'Michael Dean was a great story-teller. An interesting man, but a man who never told us the truth. As his Counsel, he told me virtually nothing. I often questioned my trust in him.'

'Why did you question your trust in him, Mr Kingston?'

Edward looked towards the speaker; one of the judges.

'Instinct,' Edward answered.

'Come on, Mr Kingston. He told you something about his past. That is why you didn't trust him.'

'I never said I didn't trust him, I said that I questioned my trust in him.' Edward replied confidently, unfazed by the judge's directness. 'I entered into his stories, his life, his personality from the day he turned up. This made me feel uneasy. It is unusual to take in a stranger without feeling uneasy, isn't it?'

'I suppose so,' the same judges replied, looking to his colleagues.

'Well then.'

After another day of twists and turns, Edward again felt strongly he was winning the day, winning his freedom and the freedom of his friends and family, almost forgetting what the General had told him, caught up in the flow of information back and forth between him and the three judges. He was doing well, and everyone in that courtroom knew it. He was defending like a professional. Competent, sure of himself, arguing brilliantly, denying the prosecution any leeway to accept any other verdict but that Dean personally took the decision not to tell anyone of his past. Come the weekend the trial was all but over. But it was not a sure thing. Edward had done his best, but this was not a balanced weighing-up of legal argument, fairly presented. This was a political decision, a decision Edward and Goscote were not privy to. Edward suspected that political interests were affecting these events, despite his confident defence. As strong as it was, it still wasn't enough.

He managed to speak to General Pickerton once again before the trial ended on Monday morning, having been adjourned for the weekend. Edward discussed his feelings with the General. How could he get to the truth? The General might be friendly enough to offer some information, if this was true.

'You should know that this trial has become a trial against Dean, as much as you.' The General was prepared to offer some information after all. 'The Federation has never caught your friend. If you are worried that the verdict has already been decided, then perhaps you should worry. They are trying you out of frustration, having lost Dean once again.'

'I have put everything I have into this, and you're telling

me...Dean is probably dead,' he offered in explanation. 'Isn't that enough?'

'Probably should be. I don't know for sure – I'm no politician. I'm saying you should be careful. I've already said everything I'm prepared to say. You've been unfortunate. That's it.'

The conversation ended and the phone clicked off. He would have to think of a way to get clear of this. He sat back in his chair for a while. Then he sat forward again, leaning on his hands. 'Think, think.' The stress of trying to think his way out of an impossible situation was worse than a Hobson's choice. There was nowhere to go here. He could not escape through the front door. He could not outwit brute force. He could not play the system, because there was no system to speak of. It was a much greater force imposing its will on a much smaller one. A terrible worry. His son Simon would be taken from him and his wife and he and his friends executed, mercilessly.

The phone rang making him leap with fright from his daydream. He picked it up. It was Chris Young. 'Your things have arrived.'

'What things?'

'From the tower block.'

'Oh, blimey, yeah. I almost forgot.' Edward jumped to his feet, happy to find a distraction.

'I'm sending the boxes up now.'

Edward put the phone down and crossed the room and left the apartment. He walked down the stairs and as he arrived at the door a clerk handed him his things, the telescope sticking out of the top of the box. He went back up and emptied it, papers and bric-a-brac spilling out across the desk. The next thing he saw he also didn't recognise. It was a small yellow parcel. He opened it with a letter opener, cutting through the brown tape, and inside was a fresh box of blue and black pens. Not brand new. They would have been there a while by the looks of them. He took one out and scribbled with it, to get it working. After a while, with spit and a few circles on the paper on his desk, it worked.

'Dean. He must have got hold of some pens,' Edward thought. 'He must have left them up there for me.'

Edward sat and stared at the pens for a while, caught in the moment. He got up and lifted the telescope and began to set it up at the window. Eventually he got it to work. It was perfect. It worked like a dream. No cracks or smudges. He could see for miles around. The new buildings were going up and he could see they would be as magnificent as Dean said they would be. A huge trench had been dug, large trucks carrying the rubble from the site. He could see giant earthmovers climbing the elevated road, and trucks returning empty for another load. Bricks and steel frames were erected right across what was Goscote, now all but gone. He could see the new building's circular shape from here. Something that would be missed without the height of his apartment and the telescope he now held in his hands. The heat of his palms and fingers smudged the grubby brass plate that lined it. He felt a little happy, for the first time since this had all started. But still with much on his mind he scanned the area, looking closely at the changes going on all around him.

As he turned to the plains he could see they were still littered with temporary military buildings, huddled round the dried-up river bed, which turned twice through the plain before disappearing out of sight. He followed the clear straight lines of the airfield and its access road, curving widely round to the major works and back behind the allotment and the fields beyond. What was left of Goscote? The wall, the garden, the hall and the Governor's house. Now he felt saddened and angry. But there was nowhere for this anger to go. He could not take it out on any of the players in this gruelling and cruel situation. His mood had flattened dramatically. Powerless, he'd have to wait an agonising three days for this verdict. He might well be dead by the end of next week. What was this all for?

Edward sat with his head in his hands, leaning forward, staring at the top of the desk. This was it. He had three days to avoid the death penalty. Three days to sort this thing out. He stood up and opened the door, passing Madeline through the apartment door and into the hall disappearing down the stairs. Madeline knew something was up immediately, grabbing

Simon and yanking him through the door, yelling after him. But he was gone.

Edward arrived downstairs breaking into a run, charging through the hall doors, past the guards. They moved in on him, and he slowed down as he reached Chris Young's office. He caught his breath, as the two soldiers closed in on either side. With his head almost touching Chris Young's door, he knocked three times, loudly, the soldiers right next to him. Close enough that their shirts were touching his. The door opened sharply, with Young grinning at him, two of the judges standing behind him in the shadows of the poorly lit office, the shutters half closed.

'Come in.' The Governor moved away from the door continuing his conversation with the judges. Edward sat down as the guards stayed at the open door. He stared menacingly at Young, as if he was about to reach over the desk and throttle him.

'You little weasel,' Edward said.

'Pardon me!' Chris Young replied, looking over at him.

'This whole trial is a sham!'

'What?' he exclaimed.

'This is a set up. The verdict has already been decided!' Edward's face filled with fury. 'You shouldn't even be here, presiding over our deaths!' Edward's face was red with fury, as he thrust himself forward in anger, trying to grab him. Young just moved back out of reach, as Edward moved round the desk.

'How dare you speak to me like that! This is justice!' Young shouted back, his neat jet black hair, becoming dishevelled, his face red. The soldiers moved in on Edward, grabbing him, pulling him out of the office. They grappled with him, as he squirmed. Then, as Madeline and Simon appeared at the door, the soldiers loosened their grip, looking back at her. Edward stopped squirming. Her presence seemed to shame these men into behaving. Perhaps it was her gentle beauty, having a calming effect. Madeline remained silent, the judges looked at Young in horror. Who knew what they were thinking?

'Throw him out,' Young ordered coldly. One of the judges lurched forward, quickly closing the door behind him as

Edward was shown out, looking closely at the huge soldiers in front of him. Once outside, Edward was forced to his knees to stop him from moving. Everyone could hear the judges and Young arguing, as tears fell from Edward's face. He wept in frustration and pain. Madeline held Simon closely as he whimpered. A senior officer stepped up and tapped the guards on the shoulder, telling them to let him up.

'You gonna behave?' the officer asked.

'Yeah,' he replied quietly.

They let go of his arms and helped him to his feet. He slowly stood up again, feeling humiliated. He glared at Madeline. He walked off into the hall, through the kitchen out to the allotment and disappeared. Madeline, frozen to the spot, just stood there and watched every step he took, unsure what to do, where to go. Everyone looked at her. The girls came over to her but she shooed them away. She slowly walked out of the hall, taking Simon with her back to the Governor's house. Hopefully, as painful as it was, this could undermine any foregone conclusion. The judges were clearly unhappy with what was occurring. Perhaps they weren't as involved in the politics as Edward had assumed.

CHAPTER TEN

The time was creeping past, as the wait tortured everyone. Edward kept his head down until midnight, when he crept in, expecting the curtains closed and Madie in bed asleep. She was waiting for him, sitting in the day room. She stood up.

'You okay?' she asked.

Edward felt like a child. He stood in front of her, as she walked towards him. They hugged each other. Edward could feel the warmth of her body on his frozen chest, arms and face, as she pressed her cheek on his. They sat together on the wicker sofa.

'How is this going to turn out, Edward? Are we heading for execution?'

Edward loosening his hold on her and put an inch or two between them on the chair. 'I spoke to someone from the Federation,' he said, carefully avoiding the mention of the General's name.

'You didn't tell me that,' Madeline sat up to listen. 'Well? What did he say?'

'He said that it was political; the trial. It's no trial at all. No basis in law, I guess he meant.'

'Really? That's good, isn't it?'

'Definitely not good, but it might be now that I have managed to speak to this guy. He said he'd do what he could for us.'

'Yeah, but what does that mean?' Madeline said, sceptically.

'This is the Federation's business, and we'll get…'

'What?'

'Whatever we're given,' he said.

Edward and Madeline stayed up all night talking, while Simon slept, often whispering in the dark. It was almost exciting, if this was the last night they had together. They talked about all kinds of things. Edward shared thoughts with her that he'd kept to himself. They talked about family and remembered growing up together, and falling in love. The good times they had. It was an important night. At six o'clock they got Simon up to spend time with him. They weren't tired. The phone rang at seven and they were invited to go and join the community in the hall all together for one last time before sentencing. When they arrived people were gathering at the kitchen hatch, just like old times. People weren't chatting and bickering though. They walked around silently, just the clatter of cutlery filling the hall as the soldiers watched. The kids in the kids' corner. Mrs Edmunds and Mr Workman sitting with each other next to the stage. Joe and May should be arguing about silly things, as they always did, their kids running riot while they snapped at each other; laughing it off a few minutes later. If it wasn't for the soldiers, Madeline, Edward and little Simon would have just watched them all morning, going about their business, trying not to think about what was about to happen. They were all deeply subdued. Everyone was scared of the outcome.

Edward took his turn and went up to the kitchen hatch, while Madeline found them a place. Joe had saved them a place at their table, and she sat nervously, while Simon played with the other kids. They smiled at each other. A moment of silence followed, and it was uncertain whether this was real or not. They made small talk. The members of the shortlist, hardly spoke once they'd sat down together. Only Mr Workman was missing from the group. The discussion that did take place was sparse and tense. They ate very little, while Simon spilled his food, and Edward mopped it up. Madeline was about to cry, Edward could see it in her face. He waited, thinking what he might say to make things better. But she didn't cry. Lucky, because Edward had no idea what to say to her.

Edward stood to take some of the plates back to the kitchen hatch when he saw Mr Workman drop silently to the floor. He went down quickly, without clutching his chest, or his head, or any part of his body. He just collapsed, sending the dirty plates crashing noisily to the floor, the spoons flying across the room so violently one of them reached Edward's feet. As people rushed forward to help, Edward bent down and picked up the spoon, adding it to his. He stood and watched as people fussed. A soldier came over to perform first aid. People cried and said he was dead. And he was. Edward was frozen to the spot for a moment, as Madeline looked at him. He looked back, put the plates on the nearest table, looking back up at Madeline briefly, and then strolled over to him. The people parted, as the soldier wrestled with him, trying to get his heart started, breathing into his mouth. But it was too late. Edward put his hand on the soldier's back, who, on looking round, respectfully stood up and made room. Edward knelt, said a prayer, and closed the old man's eyes. He had been spared the worst. He was gone. More medics arrived and they took Mr Workman away on a stretcher, as people wept. Edward looked round to see everyone staring directly at him. He felt he should speak to them.

'This is a tough time. As dramatic as it is, we need to focus on today. Please stay calm, and let's hope we all have a chance to speak to one another soon, because tomorrow we'll be given our verdicts. I love you all. We are all good people, and we will survive to say hello to each other every morning, as we always have.'

'Thank you, Edward,' Mrs Edmunds said.

'I will let you all know about Mr Workman this afternoon, so please can we meet again in here at three.'

There were a few nods among the crying. But everyone knew Mr Workman was definitely dead. They would gather to organise a funeral instead.

Edward returned to Madeline. He wanted to say more, but he couldn't. It wouldn't be right.

'Is he dead?' she asked anxiously.

'I'm afraid he is,' Edward replied quietly looking to see who was listening.

'Oh. This is just…' she let out a sigh.

'Too much?' Edward suggested.

'Too much.' Madeline did begin to cry now. She ran out of the hall into the ladies' bathroom. Edward turned and picked up Simon and hugged him, who seemed blissfully unaware of the tension in here and then followed Madie to the bathroom, waiting at the door.

'With all we went through with Mr Workman. He propped up one governor after another. He was our elder, our spiritual leader, our true governor. And he goes like that!' Madeline squawked angrily from the bathroom, as Edward held open the bathroom door, his arm aching. She wiped her eyes, checking the mirror. But as much as she tried the tears kept coming as fast as she wiped them away. Eventually she settled down and Edward and Madeline decided they'd stay in the hall for the rest of the day, to be on hand. Neither of them wanted to be cooped up in the Governor's house away from everybody. Away from being there to help, to console, to advise. Throughout the morning, Edward wondered why he hadn't seen Chris Young passing through. He hoped he'd gone, as he ought to. But unsure, he didn't want to hope. It was too hard to imagine everything would turn out alright, when all the signs were bad. His mind moved from him to Mr Workman, to the verdict, the death sentence, Sheila and Dean. Dean? What had become of him, now he'd landed them in so much trouble? Then back to Mr Workman, and then Madie and Simon. Over and over, all the issues, sending him through waves of worry, panic, anger and revenge, back to a calm acceptance of his fate. Wanting to know why all this was happening, knowing that the answers may never come.

It was going to be a long day. Madeline snuck off for a sleep at lunchtime, as people came and went. Edward dozed in his chair, every now and then, being woken by soldiers, kids, or a door slamming. By half-past two he was immediately disappointed to see Chris Young, shaking him to wake him up. Mr Workman had indeed passed away and, given the circumstances, a priest had been sent for, and a funeral had been arranged for three. All this just added to the tension.

'You've not been fired then?' Edward said in a sleepy voice.

'No, I haven't, as you can see.'

'You won't get away with this. I'm not an idiot.'

'Edward, I know you're no fool. But this isn't about being smart. It's about what you did. Who you helped.' He jabbed his finger in time with his words, to taunt him further. He stood up and walked off quickly, disappearing into his office, on the other side of the hall, soldiers closing the door behind him.

Edward sat back and closed his eyes for a second, and then opened them again, seeing a priest walk in. He stood up. 'Mr Workman,' he said to himself and walked confidently over to greet the minister, his shoes tapping loudly across the empty hall. The priest greeted him.

The funeral went as well as could be expected. Edward, distracted by the looming verdict, kept one eye on the priest as he read out the lesson and the sermon, the tributes, and a few words of condolence, and the other eye on the clock, as it ticked past. By four it was over. They decided to cremate him, but were told that he could not be cremated on site. This meant his body was taken from them to be cremated which upset everybody. He'd truly been Goscote's statesman. A man for all people. He would be sorely missed, not least by Edward, who desperately searched for the leadership skills he needed to get through the torture of these spurious allegations. He hoped they would be understanding enough to return his ashes to them, so they could be kept somewhere good. Somewhere quiet where people could pay their respects.

Edward thought about his father, while he sat and listened to the priest. His father was a strong, vibrant man, with clear leadership skills, and a decisive manner that earned him respect, if not fear. A man who knew what needed to be done and when. That weasel behind him, he could see him over his shoulder if he were to look, pretending to be Goscote's friend, could not place himself in that category. He would tell the others about Dean when this was over. He wasn't sure what the others knew. Edward kept so much to himself. It had become second nature to hold back. Keep the truth hidden inside him, until he had no choice but to reveal it.

Finally, they retired to the Governor's house and this time they slept a little, closing the shutters in the office, the curtains in the day room and the bedroom, and the large double doors onto the veranda. A constant stream of low light came in, incongruous to the political battle being fought over them by the Federation. Incongruous to the cloud that blighted their lives.

The morning came eventually. Exhausted the town came out from their rooms. At nine o'clock Goscote gathered once more in the Town Hall. They were asked to stand as the judges came out. The judges sat down and read out the verdict, as if some lottery result; their lives in the balance. As he looked round, Chris Young was missing. Fingers crossed, this was a good sign.

'The verdict has been decided, by this panel, and it will be passed into law, as from today, that the people on list A will be released without charge, immediately after this hearing.' The first long list was read out. Those already selected. No surprises there, Edward's ear listening for Sheila's name, as it passed.

'Those in list B will be held here under house arrest within the confines of the hall, the Governor's residence, and the tower block, for a period of no longer than thirty years.' A sigh of relief was heard. So no death or prison sentences. They looked shocked at this unexpected result. Now for the final list. The inner circle. Edward's fate. For what became known as the kill list.

'List C will also be held under house arrest, within the confines of the hall, the Governor's residence, and the tower block, for life with no option for release.' A mixed reception. 'There will be no appeal granted for any of the sentences. All children will remain with their parents until the end of sentences.'

There was silence in the hall. No one quite knew why it had gone this way. People looked at each other, as a murmuring rippled across the hall, as Goscote took in the verdict and the sentence, relieved that they weren't going to be executed, but confused as to this strange outcome, not quite knowing what to make of it yet. Edward was sure this was Federation politics. Very little to do with real crimes, real penalties. The judges rose and the people in the hall rose.

Edward suddenly realised that they were going to be confined here, indefinitely. No appeal. No contact with the outside world. Most would die here. A great sense of panic and terror passed through his mind, as his mouth fell open, his face drained white; his bleak future becoming clear.

He jumped from his seat. 'We're not going to die in here!' Edward's sharp voice filled the hall. 'You can't condemn us!' He climbed over the desk towards the judges as the soldiers rushed him, with his furious eyes, his rage. 'This is your problem, not ours! You find Dean!' he jabbed his finger violently towards the judges as they pulled away in shock, looking spooked by his angry reaction. Madeline was horrified, as the soldiers held him back. 'This isn't over!' his voice strained, loud, enraged. The whole town could see his anger, a near suicidal rage against the Federation judges.

'We're not going to be executed, Edward! Stop! You've done it. You've done it. Be happy. Be pleased,' Madeline cried as she grappled with him, in among the soldiers stopping him from jumping onto the stage and physically hurting these men who had condemned them.

He backed down, his breathing laboured, his face filled with sorrow and exhaustion. Prompted by Madeline, he looked round, to see some relieved faces, some sad, mostly confused. It was a mixed blessing. No leave to appeal. No right to appeal. And what of Chris Young? Edward got up and went over to his office. It was empty. He walked out through the double doors into Broad Street quickly, before he missed his chance, to look the judges in the eye. As they left three separate cars passed him, the three judges seated in each one; each one respectfully nodding at him as the cars swept through the gates.

A brief goodbye was held, as the families prepared to leave. Those chartered for release had half an hour to pack and say goodbye. The soldiers stood guard, shouting at the convicted to stay away from those leaving. Tears flowed as the two groups of people were kept apart by a human corridor of soldiers. Edward just stood back and watched, finding it difficult to stop the tears. Madeline cried uncontrollably next to him. The people fought to get through the lines, knowing this would be the last time they'd see each other. They were wrenched apart. The grief was unbearable. This was a huge injustice and nobody could do anything about it. They inched past the gateposts and sped away leaving them behind. The gate was slowly closed, and that was it. It was over. Edward might never know of their fate and they would never know of his. He could only trust they would be looked after.

He glanced at the old buses, still parked in the same place outside the hall, rusting engine parts strewn across the street. He looked back and saw the soldiers had gone from their stations, the people standing round in clusters, their arms crossed, their faces sullen. Heads were bowed, and the air was crisp in its silence. Suddenly suspicious of why the soldiers had left so suddenly and completely, he moved back into the building to the Governor's office in the hall, and picked up the phone. It was dead. He went back outside to the gate to speak to the soldiers, but they were out of reach; the gate was several metres high, with no hatch in the gate, no access to the guards at all. He looked up to see them in the watchtowers, which had gone up overnight. All he could see were cameras pointing down at him, like vicious meddling eyes. He called up to the guards but they did not answer, coldly ignorant of his obvious presence below them. This was it. This was their sentence. The very same thing that had drained the lifeblood from this town was now going to be used to punish them for a crime, unidentified; for a political goal no one could define.

He spent all afternoon pacing up and down ranting to anyone who would listen, about how to beat them. He felt responsible for allowing it to happen, seeing the whole time where all the activity of the General and others was heading. Impotent to do anything constructive, except to save Sheila and the baby and the other members of the town, he was devastated and angry. By nightfall, he finally climbed the stairs to his apartment to spend some time thinking, his eyes heavy with tiredness. Everyone had gone to bed, tired of negotiating with him. Exhausted by his endless examination of the events. He would miss everyone that escaped, especially Joe and his family. He fought back tears with his sleeve, rubbing his eyes to refocus. He then slept soundly on the sofa, like a scolded child, having cried himself into exhaustion. Madeline stayed out of the way and tried to get some sleep in the next room with Simon next to her for comfort and safety.

Eventually Edward got up and entered the bedroom. He stood over her for a few seconds, before she half opened an eye and looked up at him. 'Well, if everyone is bored of listening to me then maybe we should tell them about Dean now?' At that Madeline got up.

'Anytime you decide to tell them what we know about Dean is the right time. I'm right behind you on this one,' she told him.

'Right. Let's call a meeting then,' Edward stormed off down to the hall and knocked on doors and shouted at people that there was a meeting in the hall. Pretty quickly the remaining people gathered expectantly and nervously in the hall. They all looked a little pale and depressed and Edward felt a little guilty for taking out his frustrations on them.

'I mmm,' he now struggled to get the words out. 'I think we need to explain a few things, that we learned just before the trial, and the reason we, that is Madeline and I didn't tell you before, was because we needed as many people as possible to have deniability going into the trial. Anyway, Dean, that is Michael Dean, was a fugitive for the following reasons. He was a government engineer, working on a government building when his father, who was a minister for the dictators Intrum and Justica, who ruled the entire American continent from Canada right down to Argentina and also vast tracks of Africa, Eastern Europe and so on. I'm sure you all remember them from your history books. Nasty pair of dictators. Anyway, Michael's father was their defence minister. In a fake coup against them, they killed Dean's father. He was then imprisoned by Intrum and Justica. He escaped with a small band of men and somehow they tracked them down and killed them. That's why he was on the run. How he managed to kill them I don't know. I don't know the exact circumstances. But not long after this assassination he managed to steal three government spy drones, which he used to keep one step ahead of the Federation and its forces. So that's it. That's why we're here, being punished for this man we barely knew.'

'Thank you Edward,' someone said, touched him on the arm as she turned and left. The others just stood in silence and looked at the floor. Edward looked over at Madeline. They had nothing to say. He guessed perhaps they might have more questions when things had settled down. For now, one by one they all left the hall and returned to their rooms in silence.

'I don't know what to say, Edward. I'm not sure what I expected', Madeline said. 'I guess they're too tired and disappointed to take it in.' They left together in silence, heading for bed. They were all exhausted.

Edward woke the next day to light streaming across the room and into his eyes. It took a minute or two to realise that there should not be this much light, and when he did realise he got up, and moved the window shutters fully across to see what was happening. The sun was shining a bit, but Jupiter was shining more than ever. The cloud was still there. He stood and stared from the window, at the spectacle, thinking that God was taunting him, making him think the unthinkable, the impossible. Then without warning the light expanded furiously, engulfing the entire sky, sending him backwards into the room seeking cover. He tripped and fell back onto his arms and back, then quickly raised his hand up to his face to block out the light. He sat and watched as best he could, unwilling to look away, as the light grew brighter and brighter. The noise of the explosion took long seconds to reach him. The ground shook, the glasses in the kitchen rattled. For a full minute there was a loud, deep rumbling, louder, deeper and more fundamental than the biggest, most violent thunder storm he'd ever experienced. But this was not the sound of Jupiter exploding. It was a mix of debris, light, heat and extra radiation, heating the atmosphere, moving the dust that had cloaked the Earth all these years, making it fall suddenly to Earth. It was the noise of a distressed atmosphere, being shocked into moving quickly, violently and en masse. The rumbling sound took hold of him for a while, his heart beating violently, pulsing its way around his thin, fragile body, terrified he was going to die, but excited and spellbound by its amazing and humbling power. Then a long pause, as if the light had sucked all the noise into it. He stayed on the floor, unable to move. Then the explosion returned, so loud it engulfed everything, as the Second Sun erupted into existence, and Edward covered his ears with his hands, sitting up where he fell, like a small child unused to such unbearable noise. The light filled the room. It filled every part of everything. Then the sky opened, rain falling in huge orange clumps. The drumming sound of the rain roared as it hit the ceiling and windows. The tin roofs of the sheds in the allotment rattled so much they were coming apart. Lightning cracked across the sky and then the thunderous rain stopped abruptly. He could then hear Simon whimpering and crying in the background. An eerie silence followed, as if every living thing had stopped moving, bleating, talking, breathing, astounded by what had happened. A momentary pause, where even the sea did not crash against the shore, or the wind sweep against the mountains. Brilliant sunlight began pouring in through the windows from all sides and a strong wind blew in, momentarily. Then it was silent again. It was a glorious event that would influence every moment of human history for years to come. A story that would be told and retold forever. Orange dust covered every surface outside, as Edward cautiously got up to peer down across the yard to see the damage and marvel at the orange sludge now covering everything, like some crazy art installation.

The cloud had shielded them from the explosion. It had slowed down the blast and dimmed its brilliant light. It stopped Earth suffering an enormous blast of radiation. Sunlight came back into their lives again, as this dark era ended. Madeline and Simon came in as Edward stood up and they looked at the world renewed. They stood in the middle of the living room and looked at each other in silence, not knowing whether this was good or bad. They moved to the window and looked out at two bright discs shining back at them. It was finally done. They could see so much of the landscape now. No longer hidden by shadows. The distant hills, the plain, the dry river bed. The birth pangs of a new star. That's what it was. That's what had tormented them for so long. Edward had once read how the weather and astronomical events influenced human history. Perhaps the rise of Intrum and Justica, the Federation of Police Authorities, and the man they called Dean, were all part of the same connected universe, and Edward a mere bit player. A victim, who had become a symbol of nature's final victory over man. Edward had truly been floored by this great astronomical event. But it was no solution. It would bring more problems, not fewer. Instead of too much darkness, they would now have too much light.

Edward peered into the new world, immediately aware of its dangers. He wasn't looking forward to seeing what new horrors it had in store. He felt a bit ungrateful, but as he leant over the balcony with Madie and Simon, he was glad to see the back of that cloud. There were things to look forward to. There must be.

Part Three: Escape

CHAPTER ELEVEN

Thirty Years Later.

Edward was getting older and wiser. He was still trapped in this micro-sized version of a once thriving town. Sometimes he could understand why the Federation would not recognise this as torture, but never voiced his opinion. He wouldn't want to give any room for the Federation to win more people over to their view. Sometimes he recognised that if Dean was never tracked down he might try and return. Or that he would have infected Edward with his particular brand of revolution. Whatever the reason was, they had set the terms of his imprisonment with no intentions of going back on the judgement. It would not be long before he was sixty years old. He'd been here within the walls of the remaining buildings of Goscote for thirty years. Edward increasingly sat on his chair staring at length through the window and off into the plains, with the mountains beyond. Perhaps he had lost hope in ever seeing a different view, but no one ever speculated on this. Some of the residents had kids, and he'd watched them grow up. Most of them had suffered some form of malnutrition and all of them some form of mental illness. The supply of food and medicine had sometimes dried up for no reason, especially in the early years when nobody cared about them. Escape plans had been hatched, and escape plans had failed. The town had been locked down from all sides. There were no building projects around them to ensure no prying eyes. The fascism of the establishment was still domineering and unshakeable. They were still up on the towers, watching them through the eyes of the guards, who were no doubt bored to distraction; only there because they'd screwed up their careers.

Helicopters would sometimes fly overhead and in recent years the road at the bottom of the allotment had got busier.

His building was falling apart and his governorship had been a mishap from the start, when he watched that cloud in the hope that their misery would end soon. It had gone many years ago and nothing had changed, except the dry heat, which bothered everyone. The buildings that had been started by the Federation had been abandoned and eventually the army engineers had cleared them away. Edward suspected it was because of them. They should be out of sight and out of mind. He knew there was a base somewhere not too far away, because the traffic that was shaking this building apart was just outside the allotment wall. He wished he could see where they were going. But this was just one of the things that drove him crazy over the years. He didn't know whether it was his age, or whether he was right to be angry. When would he gather the people in the hall for one last time and tell them it was time to go? To leave this place for good. He would fantasise about standing to watch all these God-forsaken buildings get demolished and cleared away. It seemed to Edward that they'd been forgotten, suspecting sometimes that a leadership change had occurred and in the confusion Goscote had been deleted from their things-to-do list. He would write letters to the leadership to remind them, but they rarely replied, except to say that their sentence had been fair and they would not be released until its end. Even then they spelled out the terms of their release; that in no uncertain terms, they would remain there at the leisure of the Federation. The fact was, through Edward's contacts on the outside, the old regime was still in place and their imprisonment would continue until they had gone. He was reliably informed that since the birth of 'the second sun' and the demise of the cloud, their power had begun to decline. Given there was still a lot of social disorder, the Police Federation had unfortunately remained in power. New forces were growing in number and power, who challenged them without being assassinated or sent to the camps, which was a huge step forward. In fact many of the camps had closed after pressure from the growing pro-democracy media. As the Federation was to the regime of

Intrum and Justica, the pro-democracy media were the only credible opposition to Federation power. Edward had long cultivated a relationship with them. In fact a pro-democracy hearing was to be held this year, and Edward hoped his case would be added to the agenda. The only other power worth mentioning was the Construction Board. They were the wealthiest individuals in society and therefore very powerful. But they were said to be 'politically naïve'. In other words, they didn't care who was in power as long as they got their contracts.

The morning began with the staff in Edward's office complaining they didn't feel safe in the building anymore. Edward promised he'd look round the site for somewhere safer. It was true though. The building would shake violently for much of the day, with wild conspiracy theories flying round the town that the Feds were deliberately routing large vehicles to the road behind the allotment wall, to bring down the house and kill off the hub of the campaign. Edward stared at the town, his eyes peering tirelessly at small changes in the view below. It seemed any activity would be enough to entertain him. Much of the time he would focus on the view and lose his mind in the moment, not willing to push himself any further into ill health. There were younger minds around him who did that now. He watched as one of the young lads, Josh, could be seen from the office running towards the back wall and picking something up off the floor. Edward followed him closely, hoping that he would bring it up to him. Sure enough he saw him running into the building and he lifted himself upwards out of his sitting position ready to wait at the office door. He leant against the doorframe and poked his right ear out to listen for Josh's footsteps as he entered the building. It occurred to Edward that the importance of whatever had been found could be determined by the speed Josh ascended up the stairs. He was coming up quite quickly. Edward determined it was something significant.

'I reckon it must be important. He's virtually running,' Edward said, with a degree of cynicism. The girls stopped working and turned towards the door to wait with anticipation, occasionally looking up at Edward's face, now concentrating in silence. Eventually Josh appeared panting at the front door, and Edward could immediately see the headline across the newspaper underneath a plastic cover: 'Rendell highlights plight of Goscote'.

Richard Rendell was a dynamic political activist who had been campaigning on behalf of Goscote for the last two years. He was beginning to get the papers interested in talking about it. Things were changing. There was a sudden buzz in the room as the paper was eagerly unwrapped by Edward. He was careful not to reveal too much, before he'd had a chance to see what reality lay behind the hopeful headline.

A voice then came sailing across the room to ask, 'What's going on down there?'

One of the girls was leaning with her head pressed against the closed window, watching the people underneath. Everyone walked across the room to the window, and pushed for a space, having forgotten about the paper, which was now folded under Edward's arm. They watched as frail people ran around randomly picking up packages from the floor.

'Oh, I'm so hungry. I hope there's enough for everyone,' Edward said, partially to himself. It was one of those times when they got extra. They still didn't know who was doing it, but Edward suspected it would just be the Federation. Rendell had always said it was a rare thing for a civilian vehicle to go down that way.

'We should go down,' Madeline said, virtually giving permission for the staff to leave. Everyone got up and as they did the building shook violently, as another large vehicle convoy rumbled past, followed by an enormous cracking sound. The floor crumbled beneath them, chunks of concrete appearing at their feet. The staff ran to secure themselves at the edges of the room. Edward could feel the floor tipping violently and stepped backwards with them, knocking one of the girls off her chair. She fell next to him, grappling for something to hold on to as she tried to stand.

'The building's collapsing! Everyone out!' Edward yelled at the staff. They all moved quickly to the door as a corner of the building fell away, the air quickly filling with dust and horrific cracking noises. Madeline was safe at the doorframe, but Josh and the girls weren't so lucky. Edward held his breath as Rose and Josh fell off, their hands slipping on the concrete and steel, cutting mercilessly through their flesh. Edward moved forward, as Madeline cried, 'No, Edward!' He stopped dead with one foot forward. Rosaline, the girl he'd knocked over, was sitting at his feet as they carefully looked for a way back to the stairwell. There was very little room and very little time. For all they knew the whole building could go. They had to move despite the instinct to stay still. The debris had hit several children below them as they scrambled to grab the food packages and Edward could clearly see the dead below him. He looked back at Madeline as the three of them stayed still in complete silence, with screaming echoing up to them from the ground. Madeline wanted to leave, but was determined to wait for her husband. She couldn't leave without him. After pulling himself together he crept slowly along the ledge and backed carefully out onto the floor of the hall, with Rosaline behind him. He blew a big sigh as he concentrated on the space between him, Ros and safety at the doorframe. Madeline grabbed Edward's hand, and they both pulled Ros to safety. There was no time to embrace and be safely reunited. Edward and Madeline ran down the broad stairwell side by side, hand in hand, with Ros behind them. The Governor's house should have been condemned years ago. Edward barely had the strength to meet the carnage that waited for him at the bottom of the stairs. Images ran through his head as he descended, nearer and nearer, almost relieved the building was so high. The responsibility rested with him to calm people down and find out what happened.

They gathered in a sorry state, with two bodies in front of them. The whole town were in shock, as mothers and fathers cradled their dead children in their arms. As they stood in silence and disbelief a very loud bang came from the wall to their right and all of them leapt with fright and moved away from the wall. Another bang echoed through the buildings, its sound bouncing off the exterior walls. Then with a final rumble a large vehicle appeared behind falling brickwork and dust and landed awkwardly in the yard, where the allotment used to be. Out of the car stepped a tall man, in his late forties

– Richard Rendell. 'Richard!' Edward yelled in delight. He came forward and shook his hand enthusiastically, with the enthusiasm returned in kind.

'Well, you're out. All of you. You've done it,' he told them. A cheer went up, before returning quietly and respectively to the two dead that now lay on the floor, lifeless, unable to take part in their emancipation. 'Oh. What happened here?'

'The building,' Edward said, lazily pointing upwards. Round the corner the building had collapsed along one corner. Richard walked round to get a better look.

'That's tragic. So tragic. I guess it sums up what happened here,' he suggested.

'I guess so,' Edward replied.

'Well, gather your things and let's get going,' he added, in a very sombre tone, the atmosphere now filled with grief and crying, parents cradling their children and the others crying and hugging them, unable to look at their dead friends, now crumpled at the base of the Governor's house.

Edward fought back tears, as Madeline looked on, Simon stood close, unable to look away – the matriarch of the group, she felt as strongly about these kids, as she did her own child. Edward stared silently at the goings on, while Richard waited patiently beside him, staring at his shoes and the floor. He looked anxious to go, perhaps expecting jubilant celebrations, not death and disaster. Eventually Edward looked away and said, 'Anything I own can stay here,' and turned to leave the compound.

'Yeah,' the rest of them mumbled. Everyone was ready to leave now, with the clothes they had on their backs. The parents of the dead kids wanted to take their children, and as several men cleared a proper space in the wall, another larger vehicle waited outside the compound. It opened its doors and Edward instructed everyone to give the parents of Rose and Josh the priority. But soon afterwards people began to wander out onto the road and out of the compound. They were free, just wandering up the dirt track, not knowing where they were supposed to go. Edward, Madie and Simon stayed close to each other, as coaches arrived and picked up the survivors. Richard joined them. He sat one seat in front of them in the coach, and like a school kid on a trip he turned round and sat on his knees and talked to them.

'We live in these wonderful state of the art buildings now. They're self sustaining, independent communities. They're disaster proof and the sense of community is like nothing I've ever experienced before. It's wonderful. You'll love it. Trust me. Just wait till you see it. It's the most beautiful place.' Richard's enthusiasm continued, as an exhausted Edward and Madeline listened, trying to feel that same excitement that Richard had. 'And, in a few months time, all of us are beginning to feel that we could have our first elections in what nine decades, since that awful cloud arrived.'

'That's wonderful,' Edward said, trying his best. He was just so tired. It was as if all his worries had been the only thing keeping him awake all these years and now he was suddenly relived of it all, the tension had gone and his tiredness was now overwhelming.

'But, I can see you're tired. I'll let you be. We'll only be twenty minutes or so.' He turned round and went quiet, before his phone rang and began to talking to whoever had called him. Madeline turned to Edward and smiled and stroked his face. They closed their eyes for a while.

Richard woke them as the building came into view. Edward, Madie and the others, began to stretch and stand up to see this enormous building, with its high sides and colourful roof, as it loomed up, it's imposing presence almost overwhelming. The coach cooed and wowed its way all the way into its entrance. As the coach found its place within the walls, a crowd waited to greet them, maybe a thousand people, gathered waiting eagerly to meet Edward. 'You've become a bit of an icon Ed,' Richard told him.

'Why?' he replied, a little puzzled.

'Because we're fighting for democracy against the Federation. And of course the Federation were the ones holding you in that place and your release is a sign that their power is waning.'

'Or changing,' Madie added.

'You might think that, but the leadership isn't getting soft

111

on us. They're having to compromise all the time to get what they want from all sectors. But we know there are pro-democracy people inside the Federation. We come from all walks of life after all.' As they climbed off the coach, the crowd erupted into applause, and Edward being shy and having spent his life inside a small compound, was a little overwhelmed. Richard climbed up on a small platform that he'd prepared.

'All of us are pleased to have Edward and his small group of friends and relatives with us. His imprisonment by the Federation is a symbol of our fight for democracy, which as we all know is being reviewed at a summit in the summer. This,' he said in a real grand standing, overblown way, pointing down to Edward, who looked a little embarrassed, 'is a sign of things to come. A loosening of power and we should take this as a sign that we will get our way!' A cheer went up and the press stepped forward. Richard spoke briefly to the press and they politely left Edward and others alone. 'Follow me,' Richard said. About twenty people walked forward and fell into a rag tag line behind him as he walked towards a little train, which was parked in a station on the edges of the building. 'Climb in,' he said. 'Watch your step,' he added.

The train shot off into the building, through tunnels and then out into large open sections with stepped rows of apartments, little streams of running water and plants all around; people walking at a leisurely pace along the pavements and children running around. Eventually they stopped and everyone climbed out and followed various officials to their individual apartments. Richard was determined to look after Edward and his family, despite not being a town official. They followed him into a lift up two flights and then into a wide corridor and into an apartment. 'This is your place. I'll show you around,' he said.

'How do we pay for this?' Madie asked.

'Oh you don't. That's the beauty of it. Everyone has a job though. You have to do your bit. It's like a commune in a way.'

'Cool,' Simon added. In front of them was a large window that went onto a large balcony. There was simple, well designed furniture and a little hi-fi, a TV and so on.

'I will order some food for you, although normally you make your own. But seeing as you've only just arrived there are kitchens that will take orders.' Madie and Edward sat down, feeling tired. 'I'll let you get settled in and then there are a few people who want to meet you.'

'Oh? Who?' Edward said.

'Remember Sheila?' he said.

'Yes,' Edward said, cordially.

'Remember she was pregnant when she left?'

'Of course.'

'Well her son wanted to come and meet you.'

'Oh. That's good, but what about Sheila?' Madie asked.

'She's no longer with us I'm afraid.'

'What happened to her?' Edward asked.

'She died of cancer about five years ago.' They nodded in silence. Richard felt a little awkward and stood in silence for a second or two. 'But her son Kevin, he's still around and he wants to meet you, if you're okay with that? You saved his life I guess.'

'Sure. I would, we would love to meet him,' Madie said.

Richard left them in the apartment. Simon was keen to look around and took himself off into the rest of the apartment while Edward and Madie sat motionless on the sofa. 'I'm so tired. I don't know what's come over me,' Madie said.

'I know what you mean. I could do with having a shower or a bath or something. I wonder what the facilities are like.' He pushed himself up out of the chair. 'I'm like an old man,' he joked.

'You are an old man,' Madie said, with a smile.

Richard arrived later that day to take Edward and the others out to the gathering press, eager to speak with him. 'I'm not dressed for the cameras,' he protested.

'Don't worry about that. This is going to be very brief. No questions and just a short statement from you. What kind of things do you want to say?' he asked, in an awkward fashion.

'I don't know. I'm pleased to finally join the rest of society I suppose. It seems to me that everything has moved on and we've been left behind. I mean look at this place. A couple of my kids lost their lives because of the trucks rolling past the house to build places like this.'

'You're right.' Richard bit his lip and stared at the floor for a second or two. 'Okay, say something like that. Anything you want to say Edward. This is your moment to say what you want to say.'

'Sure,' he answered. They walked off down the corridor and across to the open space in the centre of the building. As they arrived, they headed for a first floor balcony, up above the crowd, who were gathered in their thousands below them. As they appealed a cheer went up and cameras flashed.

'Welcome everybody,' Richard said in a loud voice, that filled the hall. 'Today, fifty-four people, fifty-four innocent people were released from a hell that lasted thirty years, orchestrated by the Federation for no discernable reason, except a sense of frustration having not found a man they believed to be a threat to their existence. The people of Goscote never hurt anyone, they never knew who Michael Dean really was. They weren't a threat to the establishment at all!' he yelled. 'And yet here we are, having sacrificed many innocent lives. Edward and his family and friends are now released and they will live here with us.' The crowd cheered, as the lights of the cameras flashed and flickered. 'Edward would like to say a few words. Edward,' he said and stood back away from the microphone.

'I am told that we are all heading towards democracy for the first time since the disasters that changed our world so radically took place.' The crowd cheered. 'If, our sacrifice, in a our little town of Goscote, now all but demolished by the Federation, served as a sacrifice that releases the world from tyranny, then it was a sacrifice worth making, wasn't it?' he asked the crowd as they cheered louder than ever. 'Thank you all. I will no doubt see you from time to time around here. Thank you.' He stepped back. Richard stepped forward and whispered in his ear.

'Excellent speech Ed. You should run for governor.' Richard stepped back to the stage and continued to speak to the crowd, while Edward and the others were pulled aside by an official.

'There is a Kevin Smith, who wishes to speak with you,' he said quietly in his ear.

'Okay.' Edward grabbed Madie and they walked back with the official. Ahead of them with a woman, and two children was a tall, overweight man, with a ruddy complexion waiting for him. 'Hey,' Edward said, and held out his hand. 'You must be Kevin, Dean and Sheila's kid.'

'Yes. And this my wife Sandra, these are my two kids, Jenny and Karla.' Edward then looked up and saw Joe, his old best friend.

'Joe!' he said and stepped forward and they hugged, as Madie spoke with Kevin and shook hands with them all. 'It's good to see everyone,' he said. 'And your poor mum has passed on Kevin. I'm so sorry. I would have loved to have seen her again.'

'I know. She spoke about you all the time.'

'And what of your father? We never found out what happened, whether they caught him or whether he escaped.'

'Oh he escaped alright. I saw him three times growing up, but he could never stay that long. Just minutes sometimes.'

'Wow. He was such a clever man. How he escaped that place I'll never know. Mind you, I never told anyone this not even Madie.' Madie looked over with interest. 'When the first soldiers arrived, I could see your father running up the old High Street as fast he could go, and he could run fast for an old man. There was a radio operator who was tracking him. I crept up behind him, and broke his radio antenna. I'm sure to this day, it gave him just enough time to get away.'

'Maybe that's what did it Ed?' Joe said. 'Maybe that's how he escaped. You never know.'

'That's right,' Edward replied.